'Nice?' he aske

Dean was confident that her answer would be affirmative, and Charlotte didn't dissemble. She had never seen the point of being coy.

'An understatement,' she murmured.

'Let's do it again, then.'

As their lips touched for the second time, she felt that, if they had been somewhere private, these first soft exploratory kisses could have only one outcome.

Dear Reader

A new year is starting and now is the time to think about the kind of stories you've enjoyed reading during the past year and the stories you would like to read throughout this coming year. As Valentine's Day approaches, why not dream up the most perfect romantic evening for yourself? No doubt it will include a sprinkling of charm, a good degree of atmosphere, a healthy amount of passion and love, and of course your favourite Mills & Boon novel. Keep romance close to your heart—make this year special!

The Editor

Anne Weale was still at school when a women's magazine published some of her stories. At twenty-five she had her first novel accepted by Mills & Boon. Now, with a grown-up son and still happily married to her first love, Anne divides her life between her winter home, a Spanish village ringed by mountains and vineyards, and a summer place in Guernsey, one of the many islands around the world she has used as backgrounds for her books.

Recent titles by the same author:

THE SINGING TREE

FOOTPRINTS IN THE SAND

BY

ANNE WEALE

MILLS & BOON LIMITED
ETON HOUSE   18-24 PARADISE ROAD
RICHMOND   SURREY   TW9 1SR

For Heather, Lynn and Marsha,
good companions on the voyage round
Kaafu Atoll which inspired this story.

*First published in Great Britain 1992
by Mills & Boon Limited*

© Anne Weale 1992

*Australian copyright 1992
Philippine copyright 1993
This edition 1993*

ISBN 0 263 77902 5

*Set in Times Roman 10 on 11¼ pt.
01-9302-55577 C*

Made and printed in Great Britain

CHAPTER ONE

WHEN everything was neatly laid out on her bed, Charlotte did a final check.

Salt-water soap; snorkel, mask and flippers; anti-malaria tablets; camera and three rolls of film; plastic reef-walking sandals; factor fifteen sun-cream; head-set and two cassettes...

With all the items on her list ticked off, she started to pack the black nylon rollbag and matching flight bag which were the only luggage she would take to the airport tomorrow. In her job as a field rep for a major tour operator, Charlotte had watched innumerable tourists grappling with large, heavy cases stuffed with unnecessary clothes. But seven years of living and working in every kind of holiday resort had taught her to travel as lightly as possible.

While she was packing, Sally, one of her flatmates, brought her a mug of coffee. Sally was a journalist working for the Press Association. Her assignments seldom took her away from London for long and she had the smaller of the two bedrooms to herself. Charlotte and Kay, a long-haul air stewardess now on stop-over in Bangkok, shared the larger twin-bedded room. As Charlotte came back to England only occasionally, either when she was on leave or, as now, when she was being relocated, the arrangement worked well.

All three were in their late twenties and, for different reasons, disinclined to change their present single career-woman status.

'Are you excited?' asked Sally, turning back the end of Kay's duvet and sitting down on the other bed to drink her own coffee.

Unlike Kay and Charlotte, she was not widely travelled. Her job was interesting, bringing her into contact with many famous people, but her holidays were spent looking after her elder sister's children, giving her sister a respite from the burdens of being a single parent.

Sally envied the others their opportunities to see the world, even if they were, as Kay put it, 'seeing it the hard way'.

When Sally asked what might to an outsider have sounded like a silly question to put to so experienced a traveller, Charlotte was bending over her flight bag, her fair hair, newly washed and silky, held back from her face by a stretchy pony-tie. Her response, as she straightened, was the warm smile which had soothed many an agitated or irritable tourist.

'I'm always excited... and especially this time. Two weeks on a schooner, island-hopping, is my idea of heaven.'

'Mine too,' said Sally wistfully. 'I wish I were coming with you. I hate February weather. Tomorrow you'll be up to your neck in a warm sea... lucky thing!'

'But you don't like swimming, and on Wednesday you'll be having lunch with your heart-throb, in his private suite,' Charlotte reminded her. 'Would you really want to swop my trip for your tête-à-tête with him?'

'I guess not,' Sally conceded. She was going to interview the film star who had been her dream man for years. 'I just hope I'm not disillusioned. Wonder what the male talent on your schooner will be like.'

'Mainly what the Americans call grey panthers, meaning adventurous pensioners, I should imagine,' said Charlotte. 'For anyone paying the full price, the cruise is quite an expensive holiday. I'm not expecting to find any beefcake on board. Any youngish guys are more likely to be taking an island-based diving course, and most of the scuba divers I've met haven't been my type.'

'I'm never too clear what your type is,' said Sally.

The three of them had shared a flat for four years, and although Charlotte had been absent for much of that time she had dated various men when she was in London. All had been markedly different and none had lasted for more than two or three dates.

'I'm not sure I know myself,' Charlotte said, with a smiling shrug. 'Maybe I'm looking for someone who doesn't exist.'

'Maybe we all are,' Sally said drily.

Twelve hours later Charlotte was sitting in the airside departure lounge at Heathrow Airport's Terminal Two, waiting for her flight to be called.

From her seat in the No Smoking area she watched a man having his passport checked; a very tall, dark-haired man in his thirties, carrying a military-looking rollbag of dark green nylon with khaki webbing straps. The official who was scrutinising the passport made some remark about it. The man's sudden smile formed a deep crease down his lean cheek and gave a glimpse of good teeth. Then he took back the dark blue British passport, like the one Charlotte had had before hers was replaced by a beetroot-coloured European Community passport, and put it away in an inside pocket of his expensively cut sports coat.

His choice of clothes to travel in was the same as hers—an open-neck shirt under a lightweight sweater under a checked wool jacket. Freshly laundered light blue jeans. Polished leather penny loafers.

Charlotte's rollbag had been checked in and was now on its way to the baggage hold of the Swissair airbus which would take her to Zurich.

As the tall man turned away from the passport controller's desk and strolled into the crowded lounge, looking for an empty seat, her first casual observation became a riveted stare.

But it wasn't the similarity of their clothing which caught and arrested her attention. Nor was he someone well-known or outstandingly handsome. Had he been that, she wouldn't have found him attractive. Her taste was for more rugged looks, and the face of the stranger she was watching combined all the features she liked. It was a bony rather than a fleshy face, with a strong chin and high-bridged nose. His thick hair was brushed back from a broad, intelligent forehead, and the eyes beneath the straight dark brows were a light piercing grey.

There was something about him, a subtle air of authority, which suggested that he ought to be flying First or Business Class, not Economy.

She wondered where he was going, and for what purpose. Somehow he didn't have the look of a holidaymaker, which was what, temporarily, she was.

From Zurich she was flying to Malé in the Indian Ocean; a return, after many years' absence, to the remote coral atolls where she had spent her childhood.

She was wondering how much the island would have changed when her flight was called. On her way out of the lounge, Charlotte passed the seat occupied by the tall man. He was reading the *Financial Times* and didn't look up.

As she began the long walk from the lounge to Gate Thirty-four, she felt an irrational twinge of disappointment that someone whose appearance she found attractive should be someone she would never meet.

Aged twenty-six, and in a job which brought her into frequent contact with the opposite sex, Charlotte had never gone short of dates or felt herself in danger of being left on the shelf. But she had yet to encounter anyone who matched or even came close to her mental picture of the man she would eventually marry. There were times, such as last night after talking to Sally, when she lay awake wondering if her unusual childhood had encouraged expectations which could never be realised.

After all, there was nothing very special about her, she acknowledged wryly. 'Average' was the description she applied to herself. And why should a Miss Average expect a Mr Wonderful to fall for her?

Partly, she knew, because until she was fourteen she had been reared by a remarkable man whose influence was still as strong as when he was alive. Her grandfather's personality and character were the yardsticks by which she measured all the men she met, knowing from the outset that they could never wholly equal him.

Ahead of her a blonde in high heels and tight white trousers showing the outline of micro-briefs was teetering along the walkway. Longer-legged and comfortably shod, Charlotte overtook her.

In spite of her wide experience of flying to faraway places, travelling had never lost its thrill for her. Other people complained about the discomforts and delays of air travel, and Charlotte sympathised with them if they were old, infirm or encumbered by small children.

Personally, she found airports exciting places and didn't even mind being stuck in them for a few hours as long as they didn't become grossly overcrowded. She found human beings less colourful but no less fascinating than the shoals of fish crowding the reef surrounding Thabu, the short form of the name of the island where she had grown up.

In the smaller lounge at Gate Thirty-four she looked at the people already there and those arriving, trying to guess who was bound for Zurich and who would be transferring to the night flight to Malé, capital of the isolated atolls which together formed the grand-sounding Republic of Maldives.

Of these passengers bound for the Maldives, only a few would be on the island-hopping cruise with her. Probably all of them would be married couples or partners, because all the cabins on *Sea Bird* were doubles, and single people had to pay a supplement which made the cruise even more expensive for them. For her the cost was reduced by her staff discounts. But she wouldn't have been able to get a discounted passage on the schooner had it been fully booked.

To her surprise, as she hadn't expected to see him again, one of the last people to have his boarding card checked was the tall man. His height and upright bearing made him visible even at the back of the line of last-comers.

I expect he's going to Zurich on business, thought Charlotte. But if so, wouldn't he be more formally dressed and carrying a briefcase instead of a rollbag?

Boarding was by blocks of seats, and she was among the first to be called. Her travelling companion, who arrived a few moments after she had taken her seat by the window on the starboard side, was a middle-aged priest who sat down without glancing at her and whose black suit smelt strongly of camphor.

Without craning, she couldn't tell where the tall man was seated. Somehow she had missed seeing him come aboard. He could be in the seat behind hers, but she didn't intend to look.

The flight to Zurich took only two hours, during which drinks and a cold lunch were served.

She had changed planes at Zurich before. Although rather gloomily lit, it was a comfortable airport with a good gift shop and bookshop where she had hoped to add a couple of foreign books to the three paperbacks in her flight bag. Reading in French, Italian and Spanish helped her to keep her fluency in the languages which were an essential qualification for getting ahead in the travel business.

However, when she and the other Malé-bound passengers arrived at the transfer desk they were told that their next take-off had been put forward slightly and the flight was already boarding.

This threw some of the passengers into a state of fluster in case the plane took off without them. Even Charlotte thought it best to forgo her browse in the bookshop.

Thinking there was plenty of time, she had been one of the last to disembark from the first aircraft. As she walked briskly to the next boarding gate, she saw ahead of her the tall Englishman. At least, she assumed he was English, although, travelling on a British passport, he might belong to some other part of the UK. That he was also bound for Malé sent an irrational thrust of excitement and pleasure through her.

Like her, he was not in a hurry, but the length of his stride made him move faster than some of the short-legged people, who were rushing as fast as their hand luggage allowed.

Charlotte saw him draw abreast of the blonde in her ridiculous heels. But instead of passing he spoke to her and, a moment later, took from her the heavy grip she had been carrying. The weight of the grip had been pulling the blonde's torso sideways. Transferred to the tall man's hand, it appeared considerably lighter.

Charlotte wondered what had prompted his gesture. She hoped it was the instinctively chivalrous reaction of a nice man towards any woman in need of assistance. On the other hand, he might be attracted by the girl's curvy figure and luxuriant finger-combed tangle of peroxided hair.

In Charlotte's observation, men travelling alone quite often picked up girls who were outside their usual range

of female companions. As did girls. There was something about being on holiday which made people discard
their normal restraints, often to their subsequent regret.

Whatever his motive for helping her might be, the
blonde was obviously going to make the most of the
situation. Her head turned to look up at her tall companion, she was making animated conversation, her
bottom wiggling even more noticeably as she scurried to
keep up.

They had come to Zurich on an uncrowded scheduled
flight, but the aircraft awaiting them was equipped to
carry two hundred and fifty charter passengers, and most
of the seats were already occupied by Swiss and other
Continental holidaymakers when the people from
London boarded.

Charlotte found herself in the same row as the tall
man. But he was by the port window. Next to him was
an older man with a beard whom she had noticed
boarding at Heathrow. Her own seat was once again
alongside the starboard window, but this time her
neighbour was a teenage boy whose parents had seats
across the aisle, in the central block. The blonde the tall
man had helped was probably nearby but not visible.

Had she been starting her new job the following day,
instead of at the end of the *Sea Bird* cruise, Charlotte
would have drunk only water or fruit juice. But, as she
had a fortnight's grace before tackling the difficulties
ahead of her, she enjoyed the red Valais wine served with
an excellent dinner of veal and mushrooms with
couscous, followed by a delicious white chocolate mousse
and Camembert.

From time to time, as she ate, she glanced past the
people on her right at the two men beyond them, who
were now in conversation.

She had seen the tall man put his bag in an overhead locker. But, even with his leg space unobstructed, it was going to be an uncomfortable flight for him. She didn't expect to sleep much herself, and at five foot seven she was at least eight inches shorter than he was.

By Swiss time it was one o'clock in the morning when the aircraft landed at Nairobi for a change of crew. Charlotte had hoped the passengers would be allowed off the plane to stretch their legs, but this was not to be.

The boy next to her was asleep. She managed to step over him without disturbing him and, wearing the royal blue stretch socks issued by the airline, padded up the aisle in the hope of being able to stand by the forward door for a few minutes to breathe some fresh air.

Several other people had the same idea. One of them was the tall man, now in his shirt-sleeves which, being short, exposed forearms which clearly didn't spend all their time resting on desktops and chair arms.

Although he was talking to one of the stewardesses in idiomatic French, he noticed Charlotte's arrival and moved aside so that she could get close to the doorway and take some refreshing breaths of African night air.

The stewardess having been summoned by some-body's seat bell, Charlotte said to him, 'What's the local time—do you know?'

He glanced at his steel-strapped watch. 'Just gone three o'clock.' His voice was pleasantly deep, suiting his powerful frame.

She still thought he looked out of place in the cramped conditions of a charter flight. At the same time he looked capable of surviving far worse conditions if necessary. The muscular shoulders, strong forearms and flat, hard midriff were all indications of a tough physique. He was the kind of man who long ago, in the Colonial era, would have been a District Officer in some outpost of the

Empire. In her grandfather's youth, he had known many such men and told her tales of their exploits.

'If we're going to be here for an hour, you'd think they'd want to extract some foreign currency from us,' said Charlotte, with a nod in the direction of the large sign—Jomo Kenyatta Airport.

The man shrugged. 'It may be that the airline pays less if they don't let us off,' he answered.

'It's not too bad for me, but you must be finding it pretty uncomfortable, aren't you?' she said sympathetically.

He smiled at her. 'I'll survive.'

She had seen at Heathrow that he had an attractive smile, but when it was directed at her it had even more impact.

There was a pause. Charlotte felt it was his turn to make a remark. The most obvious one was to ask where she was going, for although the destination on their tickets was Malé it was unlikely any of the passengers would be staying there. They would all be dispersing to the islands leased by the Republic's government to Maldivian and foreign tour operators.

Perhaps he wasn't interested in where she was going. Although he had responded civilly to her overtures, he might prefer women who waited for men to approach them. Or he might have a wife and be uninterested in other females unless, like the blonde with the heels, they needed a helping hand.

Without speaking again, Charlotte returned to her seat.

After the movie was shown, most of the reading lights remained off while, huddled under thin orange blankets, people tried to sleep.

One light in Charlotte's row remained on all night, the beam shining on the seat of the man with the beard.

It threw enough light for the tall man to read, but eventually he folded his arms across his chest, closed his eyes and appeared to doze. His neighbour continued to read, regardless of the fact that his light was not helping the people around him to rest.

Charlotte slept in short snatches, half regretting that she hadn't accepted the sleeping tablet offered to her by Kay before she had left on the long-haul to Sydney via Thailand.

The father of the boy next to her was snoring, and the boy had taken off his trainers. Either they or his socks smelt cheesy.

Charlotte smiled to herself at the thought of the grumpy moods in which some of her fellow passengers would land in a few hours' time. Overfed and under-slept, they would need to be handled tactfully by the reps meeting them.

Her thoughts reverted to the new job she was starting in a fortnight's time. Recently the company she worked for had been taken over by another firm, and since then the grapevine had been buzzing with rumours that it wouldn't be long before, as with most mergers, jobs were axed and heads rolled.

She hadn't much fear of being sacked herself. But it had been clear for a long time that the holiday trade was changing and tour operators would have to adapt to the demand for new kinds of vacations.

The company she had worked for since leaving school had been taken over by Jardine Latimer, an organis-ation which, over the years, had steadily expanded, gaining the ground lost by more complacent tour op-erators until now it was the undisputed leader of all the British operators.

It was still a family-owned firm and the present chairman of the board was a direct descendant of the founder. Charlotte was hoping the new boss would be more enlightened than the board he had bought out in his attitude to appointing women to senior executive positions.

Knowing from experience that once people started bestirring themselves there would be long line-ups for the six washrooms, she went to brush her teeth early.

She had just returned to her seat when she saw the tall man coming back along the other aisle, a wet pack in his hand and no overnight stubble shadowing his jaw. As he climbed over his neighbour, who had finally fallen asleep, Charlotte saw that he had changed his trousers for shorts and knee-socks of the kind worn in Sydney and Bermuda to give shorts the dignity appropriate on semi-formal occasions.

Perhaps he *was* staying in Malé, not on business in the commercial sense but in some official capacity to do with government, or perhaps the legal profession.

Presently hot towels were distributed by the cabin crew. The towels were soon followed by breakfast trays bearing slices of spinach quiche with ham and hot bread rolls.

When the pilot announced that they would shortly be flying over one of the atolls, the boy next to her leaned across her to see it. A few moments later they saw what had once, in her first years at boarding school, been a sign that she would soon be reunited with the only man she had ever truly loved: the familiar emerald green patches where the ocean was shallow.

In the centre of some of the patches a bank of sand was emerging. In others an island had formed bearing scrubby vegetation which sometimes included the green mops of a few palms.

The vivid colours, the shadowy outlines of the reefs, brought sudden tears to her eyes. She blinked them back and swallowed the lump in her throat. Perhaps it was foolish to feel so emotional about them, but this scattering of islands far out in the Indian Ocean was the place she still thought of as 'home'.

Outside the airport building, but still in the shade of its portico, Charlotte and the rest of the cruise passengers were taken in charge by a cheerful Australian girl.

When she had ticked all the names listed on her clipboard, she said, 'Welcome to the Maldives, ladies and gentlemen. I expect you're all tired from the long flight, but you'll soon be able to relax on the island where *Sea Bird* is berthed. I've just seen off the group who were aboard her before you, and they all said it was the best holiday they ever had. I'm sure you'll tell me the same thing at the end of your trip. Right now the schooner is being serviced ready for you to go aboard this afternoon. Lunch will be served on the island and, if you want, you can swim there and have your first snorkel. Or just rest in the shade and sip a long cold drink. It's only a short walk to your ferry to the island, but who would like help with their luggage?'

'I need help,' said the blonde in high heels.

While their luggage was being checked by Customs, Charlotte had noticed that, although all the passengers had been warned that the baggage space on the schooner was extremely limited, the blonde had brought a large suitcase almost too heavy for her to heave off the conveyor belt. And the tall man had not been on hand to help her.

'No problem, Ms Baker,' said the Australian. 'Anyone else want a porter?'

As they walked the short distance to the quay where the ferry *dhonis* berthed, Charlotte hung back a little in order to cast an eye over the people who would be her close companions for the next two weeks. Experience had taught her that, although it seldom took long for difficult people and troublemakers to identify themselves, it was often impossible to tell who would turn out to be the nicest members of a group, or the ones who behaved most sensibly in an emergency.

In her very first job as a trainee courier on the Costa Blanca in Spain she had learned not to judge by externals. It could be that Ms Baker, in spite of her taste in clothes and her failure to read the travel information sent to her, had sterling qualities under the dizzy blonde surface.

The *dhoni* waiting for them was designed for the use of tourists, although not to the extent of having seats on deck. The passengers had their luggage stowed in the cabin, but, in order to have a good view, had to make themselves comfortable on its roof, protected from the sun by an awning.

Charlotte, who remembered long, rough passages to the outer atolls with her grandfather, was soon comfortably settled with her flight bag as a back rest and her head-set in place.

At this early stage of the holiday, she didn't want to be drawn into introductory conversations with the others, but preferred to listen to music. And to look at the familiar seascape of near and far islands and white clouds drifting across a blue sky above a darker blue ocean; an ocean stretching from the east coast of Africa to merge with the Andaman Sea off the western shores of Thailand and Malaysia.

Once the *dhoni* was moving, the burning heat of the equatorial morning was tempered by pleasant sea breezes. Only when they crossed the waves left in the wake of another *dhoni* did the ferry bounce about, causing Ms Baker to give a squeak of surprise.

She had removed her high heels and was sitting with her feet and legs in the sun. Her toenails were painted fuchsia pink and there was a gold chain round her left ankle. Her skin was lily-white and didn't appear to have any sun-cream on it.

Charlotte, who had seen holidays ruined for people who disregarded tour operators' warnings about the strength of the sun in the Caribbean and other popular resort areas, knew she couldn't keep silent while the girl burned herself. Although reluctant to speak, she was about to say something when another woman, sensibly dressed in a navy cotton skirt and a short-sleeved gingham shirt, did it for her. After rubbing sun-lotion on her own face and arms, she offered the bottle to Ms Baker.

Charlotte was not the only person to avoid being drawn into conversation. The man with the beard—whom the Australian rep had addressed as Professor Paddington— was reading the book which had kept him absorbed most of the night. And the tall man, whose surname was Richmond, was listening to a tape on one of the expensive head-sets Charlotte had been meaning to treat herself to for some time.

She wondered what he was listening to. He was not wearing sunglasses and his eyes were narrowed against the bright light. With his colouring and olive skin he would be the first in the group to achieve a good tan.

She remembered the deep mahogany of her grandfather's skin, his thick silver hair and his blue eyes. She remembered what it was like to be loved and protected and understood. Would she ever find someone else to love and be loved by?

The world was full of men, and some of them were attractive and found her attractive. But mostly they wanted a casual affair, or a trial run, or a settled life in suburbia with her being a combination of housekeeper-nanny-psychiatrist. None of them offered what she wanted: a lifetime of love and unswerving fidelity, laughter, adventure. Perhaps it was too much to ask.

* * *

Their first sight of the vessel which was to be their home for the next fourteen days came as the *dhoni* drew near the resort island where they were lunching.

Mr Richmond had the first close-up view of *Sea Bird* because he had brought a small pair of field-glasses with him.

Seen from a distance at her mooring inside the reef, she looked an attractive vessel, with her white hull and green and white awning.

As the *dhoni* negotiated an S-bend channel through the reef, people could be seen sitting in a palm-thatched beach bar built out over the water. Four young men were playing with a frisbee. And half a dozen dark-skinned men, who might be islanders or immigrants from Sri Lanka or Bangladesh, were waiting on the jetty to help with the newcomers' baggage.

Charlotte and Mr Richmond both had the same intention: to let everyone disembark before they went ashore. Because he hadn't been friendly at Nairobi last night, she said, 'Thank you,' but didn't smile as he stood back for her to precede him.

One of the porters offered a hand to assist her, and although she didn't need help to step from the deck to the jetty, she smiled and said, '*Shukaria*' and let him take charge of her rollbag. She didn't need help with that either, but guessed he needed the tip.

As she followed him along the path from the jetty to the reception building, Mr Richmond came alongside her.

'What was that word you used?' he asked.

'*Shukaria* . . . thank you. I usually try to mug up a few basic civilities before coming on holiday.'

She wasn't going to let on that she had spoken Dhivehi, the language of the Maldives, from babyhood and could also write the script called Tana.

'Good idea,' he said.

He had not surrendered his bag, she noticed. Was that because he didn't want to shell out a dollar, or because he saw no reason to let other people do things he could do for himself?

In the open-sided reception lounge they were offered papaya juice in tall glasses decorated with white frangipani flowers, and small slices of coconut. A pretty Maldivian receptionist who spoke excellent English handed out beach towels and vouchers for lunch in the dining-room, and explained that they could leave any valuables in the office safe and there was a strong-room for luggage they didn't wish to take on board.

She looked at their assembled luggage and pointed to Ms Baker's suitcase. 'There will not be room for that large case on board, but it will be quite safe here.'

At that point she was called away.

'What does she mean?' said Ms Baker. 'I have to take my case on board—it has all my clothes in it.'

The grey-haired husband of the woman in navy said, 'You won't need many clothes on board. Just a couple of pairs of shorts and one or two T-shirts.'

The blonde looked horrified. 'Two pairs of shorts...for two weeks!'

His wife said, 'They'll dry in no time, pegged to the rails. Didn't you notice the crew's washing hung out to dry?'

'I'm not planning to spend my time washing. They can go in the machine when I get home,' said Ms Baker. 'All the cabins are doubles, aren't they? There'll be plenty of room for my case on the bunk I'm not using.' She had an afterthought. 'And what about the luxury islands and the discos? We'll have to dress up for those.'

The woman in blue said pleasantly, 'Well, discos aren't really our scene. We'll leave those to you younger people.' She turned with a smile to Charlotte. 'I'm Janet and my

husband is Bill. I don't think we need bother with sur-
names, do you?'

When Charlotte had given her first name, Janet turned
to the Professor, who was again deep in his book.
Undeterred, she touched his arm and said, 'We're ex-
changing first names...if you have no objection to being
informal?'

'Only on the grounds that I dislike the name my
parents inflicted on me. I prefer what my students call
me, which is Prof,' he replied.

Mr Richmond's first name was Dean. Having given
it, he said he was going for a swim and went off to
change.

Charlotte had put one of her swimsuits in her flight
bag, and it wasn't long before she was up to her neck
in the sea, which was as clear as glass and the temperature of a lukewarm bath. Like a bath, it didn't take
long to relax her and make her forget the discomforts
of the long flight. But after a vigorous swim and a short
time floating on her back she returned to the shade of
the trees growing behind the beach.

While she was drying herself, Liz, the Australian rep,
came up to her.

'Enjoy your swim?'

Charlotte nodded and smiled. 'The perfect remedy for
jet-lag!'

'Where's Mr Richmond? Is that him out there with
the snorkel?'

'Not as far as I know, but it could be.'

'You haven't had a tiff with him, have you?' the other
girl asked.

'A tiff?' Charlotte echoed blankly.

'It happens. That long flight from London jangles
some people's nerves, and he's a very big man to sit
squashed up for hours.'

'Yes, he is, but he seemed to survive it pretty well. He was in the same row as I was. We had the window seats.'

'You weren't seated together?' Liz exclaimed. 'Oh, isn't that too bad! The cabin crew should have fixed that.'

'We didn't want to sit together. We don't know each other,' said Charlotte.

'You don't? Oh, my God, that's worse!' Liz gave a groan and struck her forehead with the heel of her hand.

'You're not making sense,' said Charlotte.

'Well, I hoped you might have had a row, but I didn't really think you were the kind of couple who'd stop speaking to each other. You both look too mature and sensible,' Liz began. 'At the same time I couldn't believe that London could have made such a cock-up of the bookings. It's by far the worst muddle I've ever had to sort out.'

In her professional capacity Charlotte had sorted out a great many muddles. She said calmly, 'What's the problem?'

'The problem is...' The Australian girl paused and took a deep breath. 'Somehow they've got you and Dean Richmond down as travelling companions. And they've put you in the same cabin.'

CHAPTER TWO

CHARLOTTE blinked in astonishment. 'Are you serious? How on earth could they possibly have done that?'

'Don't ask me. A computer error, I suppose.'

'There's no such thing as a computer error,' Charlotte retorted crisply. 'Computers can't make mistakes. It's the people who use them who do that.' Then, feeling her tone might have been too caustic, she added, 'I realise it's not *your* fault, Liz, but you're the one who has to sort it out. What are you planning to do?'

'There's not much I can do, is there? As far as I can see the only solution is if you'd be willing to share a cabin with Ms Baker.'

'No,' said Charlotte, without hesitation. 'Sorry, but definitely not! And even if I were willing, I doubt if she would be. She wants the spare bunk in her cabin for that enormous suitcase. You'll have to ask Mr Richmond to share the Professor's cabin. Or the Professor to share with Mr Richmond.'

Liz looked rather dashed by this forceful dismissal of her suggestion.

'OK...if you're really adamant about not sharing with her, I'll have to tackle the two men.'

'I'm adamant,' Charlotte confirmed. 'Had that rather nice woman called Janet been here on her own, I could imagine sharing with her. But not with the Baker girl. The only things we have in common are our sex and our nationality...not enough to make sharing a small cabin for two weeks bearable. I don't suppose the men will like it, but they won't get on each other's nerves as badly as we would.'

Liz agreed that she might be right. 'I'll go and talk to them. Let's hope I'll have the problem sorted out before lunch.'

There were showers in the public washrooms where Charlotte was able to rinse the salt out of her hair.

Sally and Kay had short hair, and wondered why Charlotte kept hers long when so much of her life was spent in warm or hot climates. Her reason was that short styles needed regular and skilful cutting, which wasn't always easy to arrange in a life spent at the beck and call of tourists. She found shoulder-length hair just as practical, especially as hers was thick and straight. For coolness she clipped it back at the nape of her neck. On the rare occasions when she wanted to look sophisticated, she put it up.

Kay used henna and Sally had streaks done professionally every six months. But Charlotte, whose natural colour was mouse-brown, lightened hers by rubbing a piece of lemon along selected strands, an inexpensive way of achieving the sun-bleaching seen on children's heads.

Before leaving London she had had her eyelashes dyed so that she wouldn't have to bother with mascara. In her experience the really waterproof mascaras were difficult to remove, and also looked hard and out of place in an outdoor environment.

Presently, pausing at the entrance to the beach bar, she saw Janet and Bill beckoning her to join them. Guessing that Bill would offer to buy her a drink and preferring to buy her own, she indicated that she was on her way to the bar and would join them in a few moments.

At intervals along the bar there were price lists of exotic cocktails, spirits, various beers and soft drinks. Charlotte chose guava juice. It came in a can, without a glass. She paid for it, pulled off the tag and helped herself to a straw from a bunch in a beer mug. Then she went to sit down with the others.

They were easy to talk to—a cheerful, contented couple who would be perfectly happy with each other's company but were also good mixers. She guessed they had been married a long time and probably had a large family of equally well-adjusted children.

She judged Bill to be in his early fifties, and was slightly surprised when he didn't divulge his occupation. It was usually one of the first facts people revealed about themselves. That he hadn't might be a clue to what he did for a living.

'We always take our holiday in the winter now,' Janet told her. 'It makes more sense than going away in the summer as we had to when the children were at school. Have you been on this sort of holiday before, Charlotte?'

'No, never,' said Charlotte truthfully.

If and when someone asked what she did for a living, she intended to tell a white lie and say she worked in an office. As most people were more interested in themselves than in others, it wasn't likely she would be questioned closely.

Liz approached. 'Don't get up, Mr Warren.' To Charlotte, 'Can I have a word with you?'

Charlotte said, 'Excuse me,' and followed the Australian girl to one end of the bar where there were two vacant stools and no one within earshot.

Liz signed to the barman that she didn't want a drink, and said, 'I've talked to both men. The Professor is willing to share, but Mr Richmond isn't.'

'Why not?' queried Charlotte.

'He just said it wouldn't work. Maybe he feels the same way about the Professor as you do about Diane Baker.'

Charlotte considered the matter from a professional standpoint. How, if she were in Liz's shoes, would she deal with the situation? Probably by sending a fax to head office, suggesting that the last of the four singles to book the holiday should be offered a generous alternative such as two weeks on the most luxurious of the resort islands. However, if Liz did that, head office would immediately spot that Charlotte's own booking had a staff discount marked against it, and she would be expected to bow out in favour of the full-fee customers.

'It's a brute, isn't it?' said Liz. 'The only thing I can suggest is that you speak to Mr Richmond yourself. Not many men can say no to an attractive girl if she turns on the charm.'

'I'm sure you were very persuasive. He didn't succumb to your charm,' Charlotte said drily.

'I'm not his type. Maybe you are.'

'I doubt it. I spoke to him on the plane last night, and he wasn't friendly.'

'He may have been uptight,' said Liz. 'A lot of people are when they arrive. Then they begin to unwind, and by the end of their time here they're different people from the tight-lipped, fault-finding refugees from the rat-race who got off the plane.'

Charlotte remembered her initial impression of Dean Richmond: that he ought to have been travelling First Class, with ample space for his long legs and all the additional comforts that people who were leaders rather than followers could command.

Perhaps his offhandedness at Nairobi had not been a reaction to her but to circumstances in his life. He could have lost his job, or a girl he loved, or been worried about a sick parent.

He could even have been hating the flight. Kay had once had a boyfriend, a mountaineer, who thought nothing of climbing vertiginous overhangs but whose knuckles were always white during take-offs and landings.

'All right, I'll speak to him,' she said.

'He's over there...feeding the fish,' Liz told her, pointing to the jetty where they had landed.

Charlotte went back to the table and asked the Warrens to excuse her. She could see they were curious to know what was going on, but she didn't explain.

Taking the can of guava juice with her, she returned to the beach, stepped out of her flip-flops and paddled through the shallow water lapping the hot white sand till she came to the jetty.

Dean Richmond was sitting on the edge of the planking, one long leg dangling, the other bent at the knee. He was bare-legged now and wearing an old pair of navy Topsiders. As she had surmised, there were powerful muscles cladding the broad bone structure of his back. He was too interested in the turmoil in the water each time he tossed in a scrap of bread to notice her approach.

For some minutes she stood quietly behind him, watching the familiar shapes and colours of the fish and thinking of Manik, the island boy with whom she had spent hours fish-watching.

Where was he now? Married with a large family he seldom saw because he was on a trading ship on the Singapore run?

As children they had been close friends, as close as a brother and sister. Now they probably wouldn't recognise each other. He might not have changed as much as she had. At thirteen he had already been halfway to manhood, whereas she, two years younger, had been immature still and, but for her long hair, could almost have passed for a boy. Which was what, at that age, she would have preferred to be.

Putting thoughts of the past aside, she said quietly, 'May I disturb you for a few minutes, Mr Richmond?'

He turned his head and looked up at her.

'Please don't move,' Charlotte said quickly, as he seemed about to hoist himself into a standing position. 'I'll sit down, if I may?' Taking his assent for granted, she sat down on the edge of the jetty about a yard away from him.

'I've come to ask a great favour of you. As Liz has already explained, they've made a muddle of our bookings, and the only way out of the difficulty is for two of the four single people to share a cabin. As Diane Baker's lumbered with that great suitcase, and she and I are unlikely to see eye to eye, I'm hoping that you and the Professor will come to our rescue.'

He shook his head. 'Sorry... not on.'

'Oh, but why not? Neither of you has a mountain of luggage, and I'm sure you and he must be more compatible than Ms Baker and I.'

'What makes you think that?' he asked.

'Well, you look as if you might have the same sort of background... schooling... upbringing. As far as one can judge, you two have more in common than anyone else in the group.'

He lifted an eyebrow. 'Do you think so? You're not very observant.'

What did he mean by that? she wondered.

She was about to ask him when he went on, 'I've already told Liz that I won't share with the Professor. You, I gather, are equally firm that you don't want to share with Miss Baker. But there's an alternative which might work.'

'What's that?' she asked.

'We could share...you and I. How does that strike you?'

It was not often that Charlotte had the wind taken out of her sails. But at this extraordinary suggestion she was silenced for fully half a minute.

Could he be serious? Was he pulling her leg? Was he making a pass at her?

Before she could make up her mind how to react, he said, 'I shouldn't think the bunks on the schooner will offer much comfort, particularly for someone of my size. I'm expecting to spend my nights on deck. If you have the exclusive use of a cabin at night, would you object to sharing it, and a washroom, during the day?'

Charlotte too had been hoping to sleep under the stars most nights. To that end she had brought with her an inflatable beach-bed. The brochure describing the cruise said that mattresses would be provided for anyone who wanted to sleep on deck. But she guessed they would consist of thin sheets of plastic foam in cotton covers and that at least three would be needed to provide any degree of comfort.

She said in a non-committal tone, 'What will you do if the weather goes off? If it rains or a squall blows up? It may be rare at this season, but I shouldn't think it's impossible.'

In fact, it was extremely unlikely, for they were now in the period known to Maldivians as Dinasha when the weather was dry and the fishing good. In Funors, the first half of June on the Western world's calendar, bad weather was usual, and long journeys between the atolls, or even between some islands, were inadvisable.

'In that case, I shall have to doss down in the saloon,' Dean Richmond said casually, adding, 'You don't have to make an instant decision. We aren't boarding till mid-afternoon. Think it over during lunch.'

He lifted the leg which was dangling and with a supple movement rose to his feet.

Towering above her, he said, 'But, if you don't agree, we shall have to draw lots, the person drawing the short straw being left behind. I daresay the tour operators will offer some compensation, since it's their fault that this has happened. But whoever has to stand down won't be very happy about it, will they? See you later.'

With a nod, he strolled off, leaving Charlotte to ponder the feasibility of his proposal.

She was still pondering when Liz joined her.

'Any luck?' Liz asked.

'I wasn't able to persuade him to share with the Professor. When I said they appeared to be on the same wavelength, Mr Richmond disagreed...said I wasn't very observant. What do you suppose he meant by that?'

'Can't imagine,' said Liz. 'Could it be that one of them's a smoker and the other a non-smoker? That's often a cause of friction.'

'They were both in non-smoking seats on the flight out. In fact they were sitting next to each other,' said Charlotte.

'Perhaps that's why Mr Richmond doesn't want to share...he found the Professor a bore.'

'As far as I could see the Professor spent the entire flight buried in a book, not talking.'

'Well, there's obviously something about him Dean Richmond doesn't like,' said Liz. 'So what do we do now?'

Clearly she had never had to deal with a problem of this kind before. For that matter, neither had Charlotte, although she had known several couriers who, working for the cut-price tour operators, had had to relocate tourists booked into hotels which were full. But that was a different problem.

'What are the crew's quarters like? Could two of them double up?' she suggested. She knew that the schooner had a skipper, a cook and three hands on board.

'There are two crew cabins. One is the skipper's,' said Liz. 'From what I'm told the crew mostly sleep on deck. I haven't actually seen them, but I should guess that their quarters are a lot more basic than the passengers' cabins. I doubt if they have electric fans. Also they're next to the galley. For people from Europe, it would be like sleeping in a sauna.'

After a frowning pause, she added, 'It looks as if someone is going to have to step down. The question is who? Maybe Ms Baker wouldn't mind if we fixed up for her a stay on one of the glitzier islands. They're none of them packed out. People are staying home this winter, or maybe going somewhere else. Ms Baker doesn't look like a yachtie to me. She might enjoy herself more on Kurumba or Bandos.'

'She might... or she might make a fuss and get your company some bad publicity in one of the tabloids or on TV,' said Charlotte.

She was thinking that, if that happened and it came out that an employee of the company—herself!—had failed to give precedence to a client paying the full rate, it wouldn't be good for her career prospects.

Before Liz could comment, Charlotte added, 'Mr Richmond has come up with an alternative suggestion... that he and I should share a cabin.'

The Australian's eyes widened. 'You're not serious? I've heard of some fast propositions, but that's a world record! What did you say?'

'I'm thinking it over. He doesn't plan to sleep in the cabin, just to use it to store his gear and as a changing-room. I shouldn't mind sharing a washroom with him. After all, the loos on aircraft and in private houses are unisex.'

'Do you think you can take his word that he'll keep out of the cabin when you're in it?' Liz asked. 'Mind you, he's a dishy guy. I was looking at him this morning, on the *dhoni*, and thinking that if I had to be marooned on one of the uninhabited islands he's the type I'd like to have along.'

'Ms Baker may be hoping for a holiday romance. I'm here for the snorkelling,' Charlotte said lightly. 'I don't believe there's any ulterior motive behind his suggestion. I'm prepared to go along with the arrangement. The only thing is…what are the other passengers going to think?'

'I'll deal with that,' Liz said quickly. 'I'll explain that there's been a foul-up with the reservations and because you and he both want to sleep on deck anyway, you've kindly agreed to share the cabin space. I don't suppose any of them will give it a second thought. If you'd ever done my job, you'd know that most people are mainly preoccupied with their own comfort and convenience.'

This was so close to what Charlotte had been thinking earlier that she smiled to herself. Aloud, she said, 'I suppose so.'

'Too right,' was the other girl's emphatic comment. 'Very few people lose any sleep if someone else has to spend the night in a hammock being eaten alive by mozzies as long as they've got a bed and their air-con is working.'

'So you don't think that, when he hears about this, the Professor will insist that Mr Richmond shares with him rather than with me?' queried Charlotte.

'I wouldn't bet money on it. He was eating sweets on the *dhoni*. He didn't offer them around. Talking of eating, it's lunchtime. You people are sharing a table. I'll show you.'

Liz led the way to a palm-thatched, open-sided dining-room with a few tables set for two but most set for four or six.

'Not many people want to eat here at this time of day. They have snacks in the bar,' she explained. 'I'll go and round up the others.'

Left on her own, Charlotte sat sipping the last of the guava juice and wondering if she had done a foolish thing in agreeing to go along with Dean Richmond's suggestion.

Near her two waiters were chatting, but they weren't speaking Dhivehi. They must be imported workers, perhaps from Sri Lanka, where a once thriving tourist trade had been badly disrupted by political and military turmoil. Charlotte would have liked to spend time there, but the company she worked for no longer sent tourists to Sri Lanka.

She was wondering how much the takeover would affect her personally when she saw the rest of the group being shepherded in by Liz.

As well as Bill and Janet Warren, there were two other couples whom she hadn't talked to yet.

Diane Baker sat down next to her.

'It's hot, isn't it?' She had changed into short white shorts and a clinging pink sun-top which outlined her enviable breasts.

'Yes, very.' Charlotte agreed. 'We're not far from the Equator.'

'Is that right?' Diane said politely, looking as if she had never heard of it.

Charlotte wondered why she had chosen this type of holiday. The crowded beaches and discos of Miami or the Costa del Sol seemed more her scene.

'Are you going to snorkel?' she asked.

To her surprise, Diane said eagerly, 'Oh, yes...I love it. I used to have a boyfriend who was mad keen on it, and he taught me. Do you like it?'

'Yes.'

Diane leaned towards her and said in a lowered voice, 'I thought they'd be younger people. This lot don't look much fun, do they? He's OK.' Under cover of the table, she jerked her thumb toward where Dean Richmond was sitting. 'I like him. He helped me carry my stuff at Heathrow. But the other one's too old, and I don't like men with beards. Do you?'

Charlotte gave a slight non-committal shrug.

'Let's hope the crew are good fun,' Diane murmured.

'They'll be islanders,' said Charlotte.

'That won't worry me. I was at school with all sorts...Indian, West Indian, Chinese. It doesn't make no difference what colour people are so long as they're good sorts.'

'I agree, but the chances are the crew will be all be married. Maldivians marry young,' said Charlotte.

'Have you been here before, then?' Diane asked her.

Charlotte was saved from answering by Liz tapping a glass with a spoon to attract the group's attention.

'Ladies and gentlemen. I have a couple of announcements to make. If at any time during your cruise you want to contact me, my base and all the resort islands are linked by telephone, and if I'm not available you can leave a message. *Sea Bird* has a radio in case of emergencies, and your captain is a very experienced skipper who knows the islands and the reefs as well as you know the streets around where you live.'

'What happens if there's an accident or someone is taken ill?' asked one of the men Charlotte hadn't yet met.

'The skipper will know what to do, Mr Neasden. You'll either be taken to the nearest resort, all of which have some first aid facilities. Or in a serious emergency he can send for a helicopter. There's a hospital at Malé, the town with the golden-domed mosque some of you will have seen as you came in to land.'

Liz paused to see if there were any more questions, then went on, 'There's been a slight hitch, but, thanks to the helpful co-operation of Ms Perivale—' smiling at Charlotte '—and Mr Richmond, the problem has been ironed out. Due to a mistake——'

The Professor interrupted her, '*Owing* to.'

When Liz looked blank, he added, '"Due to" is slipshod English. The correct form is "owing to" whatever the cause of the problem was.'

'Oh, I see...sorry, Professor.' Liz grinned at him. Broadening her accent, she said, 'You have to make allowance for us Aussies. We're an ignorant shower, but we mean well.'

Charlotte heard a laugh and turned her head in time to glimpse the white teeth she had admired when Dean Richmond was having his passport checked at Heathrow.

'Anyway, *owing* to a mistake made by someone in London,' Liz continued, 'we found we had an extra person...or not enough cabins, whichever way you like to look at it. But as Ms Perivale and Mr Richmond were planning to sleep on deck anyway, they've kindly agreed to stow their gear in the same cabin and share the washroom that goes with it. They're both being jolly good sports in the best British tradition.'

It was Charlotte's turn to laugh. She felt sure Liz was gently sending them up. Had it been the Australian girl who was coming aboard instead of Diane, she would have been happy to share with her.

'You're taking it in better part than I would,' said the man named Neasden to Dean Richmond. 'If I were you, I'd demand compensation. These travel companies get away with murder! There's no excuse for these mix-ups. A man I know booked a holiday in the Canaries. He found himself in a hotel next to a building site, with pile-drivers going day and night.'

'Oh, Stanley...' his wife said faintly.

He ignored her and launched on a tale of the disastrous holiday endured by his acquaintance which, even if true, was not what most people wanted to hear on the first day of their own holiday.

A wet blanket, Charlotte decided. She had met people like him before. Definitely *not* a good sport. In fact, Stanley Neasden could probably be relied on to find fault with everything.

Beside him, listening to an anecdote she had undoubtedly heard many times before, his wife took nervous birdlike sips from her spoon, for by now they had all been served with a bowl of vegetable soup.

The third couple looked much jollier than the Neasdens. Charlotte heard them introduce themselves to Bill and Janet Warren, by whom they were sitting. Their names were Vic and Olly, short for Olive. Vic was a London taxi-driver and Olly, a plump brunette, worked at a West End hair salon.

The soup was followed by fried chicken with rice, and for pudding they were given tinned apricots and custard.

'The brochure did say not to expect *haute cuisine*,' said Vic, with a wink at Liz, as this was set before him. 'Still, once aboard the lugger I expect we'll get some good fish.'

'The lugger? I thought it was a schooner,' said Olly.

'"Aboard the lugger" is an expression, and you mustn't go calling a boat "it" or you'll be getting a rocket from the Professor,' Vic told her, chuckling. Addressing the older man, he said, 'Boats are female. Isn't that right, cock?'

Charlotte flicked a glance at Dean Richmond. His face remained expressionless, but she saw his jaw muscles tighten and knew he was laughing inwardly.

The Professor said, 'That is correct.'

Whether he was put out by Vic's cheery familiarity was hard to say. That he took a pedantic view of minor grammatical errors didn't mean that he stood on his dignity. And if he did, it wouldn't worry Vic, thought Charlotte. She had always found London taxi-drivers a particularly nice breed of men: kind, shrewd and amazingly laid back considering the stresses of their job. She had an instinctive feeling that Vic's presence on the cruise was going to be as beneficial as Mr Neasden's would be blighting.

Lunch ended with coffee served with jugs of diluted condensed milk. The half-forgotten flavour reminded Charlotte of how strange and nasty fresh milk had tasted when she first went to school in England.

Her mind was far away, reliving the past, when Diane gave her a nudge. 'A penny for your thoughts.'

It was an inept remark to make to a stranger, but obviously meant to be friendly. Charlotte smiled and said, 'Sorry, I didn't mean to go off in a dream. Where do you come from, Diane? Did you have a long journey to get to Heathrow yesterday?'

'Not too bad. I live near Ipswich. What about you?'

'I share a flat in London,' said Charlotte. 'Have you always lived near Ipswich?'

Diane was still explaining her domestic background when people began to leave the table.

As soon as Dean Richmond had moved out of earshot, she broke off the history of her life to say, 'You must be feeling chuffed, aren't you? I mean, it gives you a head start. Sharing a cabin with him!' It was said in a tone of friendly raillery tinged with a hint of rivalry. Diane confirmed this impression by saying, 'But it was me he noticed first. If he's the only guy of the right age around, I'm not going to stand back and say, "He's all yours, love." Not likely! I didn't come all this way, and spend all that money, to look at the moon by myself.'

Charlotte laughed. 'What makes you think he'd look at either of us? He may be saving himself for the beautiful *signorinas* at the Italian resort islands, or a Nordic diving instructress. There's a lot of competition around.'

'So there may be, but not on the spot, like you and me,' said Diane. 'Two birds on board is worth half a dozen ashore. I'm betting he'll pick one of us.'

Charlotte wanted to say, You're welcome to him. I don't want him. But she knew that it wasn't quite true. She was not as indifferent to Dean Richmond as she would like to be.

What she said was, 'I don't think a cruise on a schooner is the ideal set-up for a holiday romance, Diane. We'll be eating our meals together, going ashore in a group. Fifteen people, counting the crew, on a schooner the size of *Sea Bird* doesn't allow much privacy. Let's follow the others, shall we? We'll be going aboard shortly.'

As they left the dining-room, Diane said, 'No offence meant, you understand? I like you. You're nice. But if there aren't enough fellas to go round, it's every girl for herself. That's fair enough, isn't it?'

'Perfectly fair. No offence taken,' said Charlotte. There was something disarming about the way Diane had put her cards on the table.

'That's all right, then.' Diane fished a mirror and a lipstick out of her tote bag and repainted her mouth. 'It's like melted butter, this lipstick! There'll be a fridge on board, won't there? I like to keep my eye-liners in the fridge. You can get a better point if they're cold. Did you know that?'

Charlotte shook her head. 'There's sure to be a fridge for keeping the beer cold.'

'I don't drink beer—it's fattening. Voddy and lime is my tipple. I bought a bottle of voddy in the duty-free at Heathrow. I know it said in the booklet they sent us that we'd have our luggage searched and alcohol would be confiscated, but I chanced it. Did you?'

Again Charlotte shook her head. 'I like wine better than spirits, but I shan't miss it for a fortnight.'

'To my mind it's not a holiday if you can't have a drink when you fancy one,' said Diane. 'I've come to have a good time and I'm not going to spend happy hour sipping fruit juice, no matter what the rules are. See you later.'

She walked off in the direction of the washrooms, leaving Charlotte thinking about her own motives for coming on this holiday.

She had told herself that it was a good idea to ac-climatise before starting her new job, but nostalgia was the main reason. These faraway atolls which, seen from the sky, looked like a necklace of turquoise beads flung carelessly down on a bed of rippled blue silk had never been far from her thoughts during the years of exile.

London was certainly not home and never could be. Perhaps in a large airy flat overlooking the Thames, the Hudson or the Seine she might find big city life bearable. But really it was the sea she needed.

A voice broke into her thoughts.

'The waves hitting the reef sound like a jumbo jet taking off.'

Dean Richmond was standing nearby, his hands in the pockets of his shorts, his grey eyes focused on the long line of white surf on the hidden barrier of coral which was the outer reef surrounding all the islands in this atoll.

'Or the drone of the traffic around Hyde Park,' said Charlotte.

Sometimes, on summer afternoons, she had sun-bathed in the park with Kay and tried to pretend that the noise of thousands of vehicles was the booming of the sea on the reef around Thabu.

'Do you live near Hyde Park?' he asked.

'Not far. We—two girlfriends and I—have one floor of a house near the Portobello Market. Do you live in London?'

'I have a pied-à-terre there. What's the matter?'

His question was prompted by Charlotte's sharp intake of breath, an involuntary reaction to the shock she had just had.

The white fibreglass dinghy belonging to the *Sea Bird* had beached not far from where they were standing. There were two men in it, one a small, thin, dark Maldivian and the other a taller, lighter-skinned man.

She had never seen the small one before, but the other she knew well and would have recognised anywhere. It was Manik, her childhood friend.

CHAPTER THREE

As HE came up the beach towards them he was speaking to his companion, and it seemed he would pass without glancing at the two European tourists.

He was half European himself. His father had been a Norwegian from an ocean-going yacht which had run aground in a June storm. His mother had been a beautiful, intelligent Maldivian girl, the youngest daughter of a *kateeb*, an island chief.

Disowned by her father for allowing herself to be seduced by a foreigner, she had later kept house for Charlotte's grandfather, but had died when her son was nine. Charlotte had only dim memories of her.

Now, as Manik came nearer, she saw that, as was so often the case with people of mixed race, he had grown into an exceptionally good-looking man. He was not quite as tall as the Englishman standing beside her, but much taller than most Maldivians, not only because of his half-Scandinavian ancestry but also because his Maldivian forebears had lived on an island in the Equatorial Channel where, because of a more varied diet, the people had finer physiques than the majority of islanders.

Passing two or three yards from where she was standing, Manik suddenly looked at her. For a second or two their eyes met. Then, as she was about to speak, his golden-brown gaze switched to the man she was with and to whom he gave a polite, half-smiling nod of acknowledgment.

42

As he and the small man walked past Charlotte knew that nothing about her had struck a chord in his memory.

She realised too that she hadn't explained the reason for her audible gasp of surprise. Somewhat belatedly she told a white lie. 'Something bit me.'

Dean Richmond didn't query her explanation, but said, 'Mrs Warren was bitten by a mosquito lurking under the table during lunch. And I noticed some people in the bar had bad bites on their arms and legs. Whoever's running this island isn't keeping the insect life under proper control. But that won't be a problem while we're at sea.' After a slight pause, he added, 'I shouldn't be surprised if the taller of the two men who passed us is our skipper.'

'What makes you think that?' she queried.

'He was wearing jeans and a proper shirt, not a T-shirt. But apart from his clothes, he didn't look like an ordinary seaman. In a man, the ability to take charge is almost as easily recognisable, but as hard to define, as a good nature in a woman.'

'Are you a psychologist by profession, Mr Richmond?'

He laughed. 'God forbid! But I know a leader when I see one.'

She remembered thinking the same thing about him at Heathrow yesterday morning.

Looking down at her, still amused by her question, he said, 'If we're going to be sharing a cabin, don't you think first names are in order? Mine is Dean. Yours is . . . ?'

'Charlotte.'

'Have you done much sailing before?'

'A little . . . on much smaller boats. Have you?'

'I used to crew for a friend with a racing dinghy when we were both in our teens. I haven't done much since then. Anyway, I imagine the skipper of *Sea Bird* prefers passengers to behave like passengers and not get in the way of his crew.'

'Probably,' she agreed.

'You like travelling, obviously, or you wouldn't be here.'

'It depends how you define travelling,' said Charlotte. 'I've never been anywhere really adventurous... never slogged across deserts or hacked my way through a jungle. I've only been to the tourist places. Have you done any real travelling?'

'Not recently. My father spent a lot of time abroad when I was at school, so I saw a bit of the world then. Sometimes he took my sister and me on trips into the interior of the countries he was visiting. They seemed adventures to us. We saw the hill tribes and the elephants working in Thailand long before they became a show for tourists, and we trekked in Nepal before the masses discovered it.'

'Then you're far more travelled than I am. I've only been to places a taxi-ride from an international airport.'

'Of those, which did you like best?' he asked.

'I liked them all in different ways. Even Spain, which most people think has been irretrievably ruined by high-rise hotels and twee villas, has wonderful empty valleys and unspoilt villages not far away from hideous resorts like Calpe and Torremolinos.'

'I've been to Madrid, but never to the notorious Costas. France and Italy are the countries I like best in Europe.'

At this point they were joined by Bill and Janet Warren, and the conversation became a general exchange of travel experiences.

'I'm going to try one of those chairs,' Janet said presently, crossing the sand to a row of four *jolis*, a traditional island form of seating with large-mesh netting, made from coconut fibre, slung from a rustic wood frame.

'They're surprisingly comfortable,' she reported, from a sitting position, as the other three strolled to join her.

Charlotte had spent hours in a *joli* on the beach at Kuda Thabu, reading the books her grandfather had brought from England when he was posted to the Maldives as one of the last High Commissioners during the period when the atolls were a British protectorate.

By the time she came into his care he had retired to Thabu, although it was on nearby Kuda Thabu—meaning Little Thabu—the islet given to him by the last Sultan of the Maldives before the country became a republic, as a reward for his services, that he actually lived.

After his death, the small fishing community on Thabu had been moved to another island and, as far as Charlotte knew, both Thabu and Kuda Thabu were deserted. Whether she had any claim to the islet, she had no idea.

It felt strange to be sitting in a *joli* again after so long an interval; stranger still to know that Manik, with whom she had once been on terms of the closest intimacy, was also here but hadn't recognised her.

Or was it possible that he *had* recognised her but had chosen to pretend otherwise?

When they were first separated, she had missed him almost unbearably. He must have missed her too, but not as much, because going to sea on a freighter, visiting strange foreign ports, having adventures, was what he had always wanted.

They had not seen each other for two years. The first time he came back to the island, Charlotte and her grandfather were on a visit to Colombo. On the second occasion, they were there, but the long separation had made her shy of him. Manik had grown much taller and she had started her periods and begun to show the first signs of developing a waist and breasts.

She had also begun to dream about falling in love, and for a while after Manik's departure she had dreamed about him. Few modern books came her way, and those she had read gave the impression that love, followed by marriage, was the most exciting adventure open to women.

Perhaps it was because he guessed the nature of her daydreams that her grandfather had suddenly decided to send her to school in England; or perhaps he had already known he had a heart condition which might suddenly carry him off.

During the terrible bouts of homesickness during her first year at boarding school, Charlotte had found comfort in fantasies in which she let Manik know how unhappy she was and he came to rescue her and the two of them ran away together.

But gradually the homesickness had abated and, wanting to please her grandfather, she had begun to work hard at her lessons and to think less about love and more about good exam results.

Inevitably, returning to the islands had revived her memories of Manik. But she hadn't expected to run into him on her first day back, nor to find, if Dean's guess was correct, that they were going to be in each other's company every day for the next two weeks.

When she had worked up a tan, and he saw her in the water with her hair plastered to her head, wasn't it likely he would glimpse the child she had been in the woman she had become? Or was his memory of that coltish tomboy now so faded that he would never recognise her?

Decisions, decisions, she thought. Already today she had had to make up her mind about sharing a cabin with Dean. Now she was faced with another dilemma. For if, in a few days' time, Manik did recognise her, he would

guess that she knew who he was and wonder why she
had kept silent. He might think she didn't want to resume
their friendship.

On the other hand, if she told him who she was, it
would be impossible to conceal from the others that she
had lived in the Maldives and spoke Dhivehi—facts
which, not wishing to be bombarded with questions and
expected to act as an interpreter, she preferred to keep
to herself.

Also it might cause Manik embarrassment. He would
know that she understood what he and the crew were
saying. And he might not want to resume a friendship
he had enjoyed when they were children but would find
a nuisance now.

After all these years, how could she tell how his mind
worked? Maybe the best thing was to say nothing for
the time being and see how things went. Play it by ear.

The cruise party and their baggage was taken off the
island in two groups, the first composed of Vic and Olly,
Diane, Dean and Charlotte.

Supervising the transfer were two Maldivian crew who,
when they had brought the dinghy alongside the ladder,
first handed up the luggage to the two men aboard.
Manik was still ashore somewhere.

The first of the passengers to board was Olly, who
clambered up the ladder rather awkwardly but without
fuss.

'You're next, Diane,' said Vic.

'Oh, my God, I don't like this bit!' Even though she
had taken off her white and gold sandals, Diane was
unsteady on her feet and clutched at him for support as
the boat rocked slightly. Seen from below, her blue satin
shorts looked even briefer as she went up the ladder,
displaying not only her thighs but the soft curves of her
bottom before she was helped inboard.

Such a display of bare flesh by a full-grown woman would have shocked the islanders on Thabu, but probably these Maldivians were used to immodestly dressed tourists and took no notice, thought Charlotte.

Her own shorts were Bermudas, and she nipped up the ladder without really needing the crew's helping hands, nevertheless saying, 'Thank you,' to them instead of the '*Shukaria*' she had murmured to the boatman on the *dhoni*.

Although not a nimble boarder, Diane was obviously street-wise enough to grasp that, unless the cabins were allocated, it would be a case of first-come, best served. Leaving her baggage where it was stacked on the deck, she shot below and, when the others followed, had already laid claim to one of the forward cabins.

'Which end rocks about most if the sea's rough, Vic?' asked Olly.

'I don't know, but it'll be cooler away from the galley. This'll do us,' he answered, dumping one of their grips in the cabin next to Diane's.

'I'll leave you to choose our cabin, Charlotte,' said Dean.

The amused gleam which accompanied this statement made Charlotte look away, unwillingly aware that her pulse-rate had suddenly accelerated. She also felt slightly breathless, and she knew what these feelings indicated.

'As we're only going to make minimal use of it, this one looks all right to me,' she said, stepping into a cabin on the port side.

It received good light and ventilation from a deck-light, but as this was above a built-in bank of drawers, the occupants of the cabin could not be seen by anyone passing on deck.

The two bunks had been made up with clean sheets and pillows. No other bedding was necessary. Indeed, even with the deck-light open, the atmosphere in the cabin was extremely close.

As she opened a taller locker to see how much hanging space there was, and how many hangers, Dean followed her into the cabin and hoisted his rollbag on to the upper bunk.

'I'll leave you to stow your gear. I'll unpack mine later. Does the fan work?' He flipped the switch of a fan attached to the bulkhead, activating a welcome current of air. 'See you on deck.' He disappeared.

For coolness, Charlotte left the cabin door open while she unzipped her rollbag and began to spread its contents on the lower bunk. The shelf on top of the drawers would serve as a dressing-table, but the few toiletries she had brought could remain in the box-shaped strawberry-patterned zip bag Sally had given her for Christmas.

She was starting to hang up her few clothes when she heard the other group boarding and wondered when Manik would appear. It seemed he might still be ashore, for, as the rest of the passengers came below, she heard the dinghy's outboard motor starting up again.

It didn't take long to arrange her belongings. The only things she left out were her books, her sketch-pad and a flat tin of aquarelles which could be used like crayons or brushed out in a soft wash not unlike watercolours. They had been a Christmas present from Kay.

Thinking about her flatmate, Charlotte could imagine her reaction to being obliged to share a cabin—even what was going to be, in effect, a day-cabin—with a stranger.

Kay wouldn't turn a hair. She admitted to being what she called a man-eater and had been having affairs of variable duration since she was sixteen. As she was glamorous, intelligent and fun to be with, she had a wide choice of partners, and her lovers were always men whose attractions matched hers. That some of them had wives didn't worry her. She had never set out to attract a man

who was happily married. In the early stages, she let the
men make all the running.

Kay, finding herself in Charlotte's present situation,
would accept it as a gift from the gods. In her view, a
holiday without sex was as disappointing as one without
sun.

'Not a lot of room in these cabins, is there?' said Olly,
leaning through the door. 'Listen, love, are you sure
you're happy about this business of sharing with Dean?'
She lowered her voice. 'I can see why you wouldn't want
to share with Diane. Her cabin's a shambles already
stuff everywhere! You're like me . . . tidy. It'd drive you
mad, sharing with that one. What I don't understand is
why the Professor hasn't offered to share with him.'

'It's been mooted, but Dean doesn't want to share with
him. I don't know why not, but he doesn't. Anyway, as
we'll both be sleeping on deck, this seems a workable
arrangement,' said Charlotte.

'Maybe.' Olly sounded doubtful. 'As long as you're
comfortable up there. I've been talking it over with Vic.
If it doesn't work out, you can always come in with me,
and he'll share with Dean.'

'It's very kind of you, Olly,' smiled Charlotte, 'but I
shouldn't dream of putting you out. To separate you
and your husband would be ridiculous.'

'It wouldn't worry us, love. I mean, in this heat and
with these narrow bunks, it's not exactly ideal conditions for honeymooners, is it?' Olly said with a chuckle.
'At our age we need somewhere like the Sheikh's Room
to get us going, but we couldn't afford it.'

'Where's the Sheikh's Room?' asked Charlotte,
amused.

'It's where Fergie—the Duchess of York—stayed . . . or
so I've heard. The island is called Kitty-something—I
can't pronounce half these names—and there are only
six cottages . . . very exclusive, and very pricey! So Vic

and me'll have to wait till we come up on the pools. If you're finished down here, let's go up and have a cold drink. I'm parched again!'

Charlotte followed her up a short steep companionway leading to the saloon, from which another companionway led aft to the rest of the cabins, the galley and the crew's quarters. The saloon itself was equipped with cushioned banquettes round three sides of a table. In a quick glance, as they passed through, Charlotte noticed a shelf of books, the ship-to-shore radio, a stack of magazines and, beside them, various boxed games and packs of playing cards.

Olly was still wearing flip-flops but, reverting to a habit learned long ago in childhood, Charlotte was barefoot and did not expect to wear shoes again, except when ashore, until their final disembarkation.

Vic was already on deck, chatting to Dean. 'We're having a beer. What'll you girls have?'

Olly chose beer. Charlotte asked for a bottle of water. She knew it was essential to drink a minimum of a litre a day in this climate. Even in European resorts where the temperature was lower, she had had to deal with tourists who had become ill through drinking lots of *vino* but neglecting to replace the fluids they had lost by sweating and becoming dehydrated.

With the rest of the party still below, sorting themselves out, the four of them sat under the awning which shaded the part of the deck which combined the functions of sitting- and dining-room.

'Where's our skipper, I wonder?' said Vic.

'I think that's him on the beach,' said Dean.

Charlotte saw Manik crossing the sand and stepping lightly into the waiting dinghy. As he stood in the bows of the dinghy as it came skimming over the clear still water, she noticed that, unlike his crew, who all had moustaches, his upper lip was clean-shaven.

As they rounded the schooner's stern, he didn't wait to board by the ladder like his passengers but came up over the stern rails with the ease of a man who had been at sea most of his life. Seeing them, he smiled and came forward, his glance passing over all four and coming to rest on Vic.

'Good afternoon, ladies and gentlemen. Welcome aboard. I'm your skipper—my name is Manik. If you have any questions or problems, please don't hesitate to ask me. I want you to enjoy your holiday on *Sea Bird*.'

'Right you are, Skipper, we'll do that,' said Vic, with a grin.

Manik's face, rather grave in repose, broke into an answering smile. Then before Vic could introduce them, if indeed he intended to, he murmured, 'Excuse me, please,' and went below.

'He seemed to speak very good English,' said Olly. 'I suppose he has to, being in charge of a bunch of foreigners. It's quite a responsibility, isn't it? Do you think it's his boat?'

'I doubt it,' said Vic. 'A boat this size costs a mint of money. I should think it's owned by some rich bloke in Malé, or a consortium maybe. What do you reckon, Dean?'

Charlotte did not catch his reply because Olly, perhaps losing interest in *Sea Bird*'s ownership, asked her, 'What protection factor is your sun-screen? I bought eight. Do you think that's enough?'

Soon after this the crew began to take down the awning. By the time the rest of the passengers came on deck the schooner was under way, her engine throbbing and Manik at the wheel steering a careful course through the narrow channel to open water.

Once out of the lee of the island, there was enough breeze for him to order the crew to make sail. While he was keeping an eye on this operation, Charlotte was able to study him.

The untidy tangle of black curls he had had when she'd last seen him was now neatly cropped and glossy from a recent wash. And the look he had had then, of parts of his body outgrowing other parts so that his hands had been too big for his thin wrists and his shoulder-bones too wide for his scrawny chest, had gone. He was all of a piece now, a man to turn girls' heads in both senses, not only in the Maldivians' islands but also in the tourist resorts.

She watched the light, almost caressing touch of his hands on the spokes of the wheel and found herself wondering how many girls had been stroked by those supple brown fingers.

When he spoke to the crew, and they answered, none of them raised their voices. Clearly they were accustomed to working together and were repeating actions which had become routine. Even so, it was done with a minimum of fuss.

A light tap on her arm startled her.

'I'm going down to sort out my gear,' said Dean.

She wondered if he had noticed her watching Manik.

She said, 'I've taken the top and bottom drawers and left the two in the middle for you. There are five hangers each.'

He nodded and bent his tall frame to step through the hatchway without knocking his head.

It was a two-hour passage to the uninhabited island which was their first night's anchorage. When the anchor was fast and while the crew were taking a line to a buoy just outside the reef, Manik announced, 'Here the swimming is good . . . not much current.'

Eager to get in the water, Charlotte told Dean she was going down to the cabin.

'I shan't be long,' she said.

Of the three swimsuits she had brought with her, she put on the plain black one-piece in which she could dive and swim vigorously without any danger of it coming adrift. She had been taught to dive by her grandfather and, at school, diving and swimming were the only sports at which she had excelled. The team games had left her cold, although she had enjoyed tennis.

Before any of the others were ready to go over the side, she was poised on the varnished rail by the ladder and, seconds later, was plunging into the seemingly cool depths below. Opening her eyes, she could see the sandy bottom, the schooner's keel and a great variety of fish.

When, running out of breath, she surfaced, Manik and one of the crew were looking down, watching her. Perhaps they always kept an eye on swimmers.

She smiled up at them. 'It feels wonderful!'

The seaman's dark face split into a broad grin, but Manik's remained impassive.

As Charlotte trod water, resisting an urge to speak to him in his own tongue, to tell him who she was, Diane appeared.

'Not swimming?' Manik asked her, seeing she had not changed.

'Not in water that deep.' She gave him the coquettish look she probably gave to all men. 'I don't like going out of my depth. I'm not a good swimmer.'

'Maumoon will take you to swim from the beach,' he told her, before giving some instructions to the other man.

Charlotte heard Diane say, 'I don't want to put you to any trouble.'

'No trouble. Maybe others not swim like her——' with a gesture in Charlotte's direction.

She climbed the ladder to dive again. As she stepped inboard, Dean appeared. He looked at her figure as revealed by the conservatively cut but clinging black fabric.

His appraisal was brief. Perhaps he thought her too thin, her breasts too small. She knew her figure couldn't compare with Diane's opulent curves when they were displayed in full detail, as they undoubtedly would be.

Dean dived from the roof of the saloon, launching his tall body into the bright air with the recognisable ease of someone else who was totally at home in the water. Charlotte delayed her own dive to watch him surface and strike out, the muscles of his shoulders and back in full play as he surged through the water with a powerful racing crawl.

'Strong swimmer, your man,' said Manik.

'Yes, he is...but he's not my man.'

He frowned. 'You sleep in same cabin.'

'No, we shall both sleep on deck. There's been a mistake in the bookings...not enough cabins for everyone. But Dean Richmond——' pointing to him '—and I don't want to sleep below, so there's no problem. We shall only use the cabin to change our clothes...never at the same time.'

Either he didn't understand or he disapproved. His eyebrows remained drawn together. Not sure how good his command of English was now, Charlotte asked, 'Do you understand?'

'No, because if Richmond is not your man, it's better you share with a woman...the one who can't swim.'

'There's no room in her cabin...she's brought too much luggage.'

'Then Richmond must share with the old man with beard.'

'He doesn't want to do that.' She searched her mind for words to explain. 'Do you understand French?'

As a boy he had spoke Dhivehi and some English, but no other languages. By now he might have picked up a smattering of several.

'I know a little bit,' he told her.

After glancing about to make sure the Professor was not with earshot, Charlotte said, 'They are not *en rapport* . . . Richmond and the old man.'

'That is what Richmond tells you. No young man wants to share cabin with old man if he can sleep with woman.'

'That's definitely not his intention. We shall both be sleeping on deck,' Charlotte said firmly.

'Maybe not your intention,' said Manik. 'But how do you know what's in his mind?'

'Because I'm not a fool, and he isn't that kind of man,' she said, beginning to feel slightly exasperated.

'All men have hunger in loins for a woman who is young and pretty,' he told her curtly.

Charlotte's crossness gave place to suppressed amusement. Where had he picked up that Biblical-sounding turn of phrase?

She said gravely, 'But good men do not give offence to good women. He is a good man and I am a good woman. There's no cause for worry.'

Their conversation was brought to an end by the others coming on deck. The Professor and Mr Neasden climbed down the ladder. Vic dived. Olly and Mrs Neasden said they would swim from the beach with Diane.

After her swim, Charlotte used the deck shower, a hand-held spray fitting attached to a hosepipe connected to a tank of fresh water. The pipe had been lying in the sun and for the first few moments the water ran warm over her hair.

It was the time of day when the sun had lost its blistering heat and it was safe to expose her shoulders. After going below to peel off her wet bathing suit and dry herself, she put on briefs and a cotton sarong Kay had brought back from Malaysia. Charlotte had used it a lot and liked it even better now that the vegetable dyes had faded to softer colours. Wrapping it round her body, she tied it in a knot at the front.

When the sea swimmers had assembled on deck, but before the beach party had come back, one of the crew brought up a tray of canned drinks. When they had each made their choice, Manik appeared with an exercise book.

'Please write your names and put down what you drink. You pay at the end of the cruise,' he explained, handing the book, which had a pencil tied to it, to Vic.

'Right-ho, Skipper. Whatever you say.' When Vic had filled in his name and marked the appropriate column, he passed the book to Charlotte. ''Spect you're missing your G & T, aren't you, my love?'

'I may have a secret supply stashed in my cabin,' she said, smiling.

'Never! You wouldn't have smuggled a bottle through the Customs. You're not the type...but I am,' he added, guffawing. 'Or I would be if I didn't have Olly to keep me in order. Very law-abiding, she is, worse luck.' He gave Dean a nudge with his elbow. 'Take my advice and stay single, mate. You can't call your soul your own once you've got spliced.'

'Dangerous talk, Vic,' said Dean. 'There may be a feminist present.'

'You mean Charlotte? Not her...no way! If she was a feminist, mate, she'd never have let you stow your kit in her cabin. You'd have been told to get lost. Ah, here comes my lady wife. I'd better give her a hoist up the ladder.'

Olly was wearing a T-shirt over her swimsuit and Mrs Neasden had put on a floral beach wrap. But Diane had taken no cover-up to the beach, and when she came into view there was very little of her figure left to the imagination by her hot pink and yellow costume with its extra-high-cut leg line and almost navel-deep cleavage.

'Strike me pink!' said Vic, blinking theatrically.

Charlotte swallowed a laugh. Even the Professor, she noticed, looked up from the book he was reading and stared at Diane over the top of his half-glasses.

Dean's reaction was a sweeping appraisal of all that Diane was displaying, but whether he liked what he saw was impossible to tell.

What Maumoon and the youngest of the crew who taken the women ashore thought of Diane's scanty suit was also imponderable. On Thabu, in Charlotte's time, all the older women had worn long-sleeved, ankle-length dresses, and she couldn't believe that things had changed much since then.

Diane gave them her flirtatious smile. 'We had a *lovely* swim, didn't we, Sylvia?'

'Very nice,' Mrs Neasden said quietly. So far, she hadn't opened her mouth unless someone spoke to her.

Charlotte felt sorry for women like Sylvia Neasden who seemed to have no identity except as their husband's wife. In her professional capacity, she had found that, in a group of holidaymakers, although they contributed nothing to the enjoyment of the group, they were never the pain that their husbands frequently were. It was odd how often meek women and self-important men seemed to go together. She could understand the men choosing women who wouldn't stand up to them, but was baffled by why timid women should choose domineering men.

Typically, Mr Neasden said, 'You'd have had a better swim over the side. But of course, if you're worried about spoiling your hairdos...' He gave a patronising shrug.

Sylvia looked crushed, but Olly was less easily put down. 'We all have our problems. You'll have to take care with your bald patch, Stanley—you could get a nasty burn if you forget to keep it oiled. Down you go, Sylvia.'

Ignoring the angry tightening of Mr Neasden's thin lips, she gave Vic a covert wink and Sylvia a gentle push towards the hatchway.

The crew came to put up the awning which they slung over the boom of the mainsail. While they were doing this Charlotte went forward and continued sipping her guava juice with her elbows resting on the foresail boom. She remembered the hours she had spent, as a child, gazing at this same view of empty sea and distant horizon, wondering about the great world that lay somewhere beyond it.

Now she knew what the great world was like, but she hadn't yet found her place in it. Perhaps this was her place.

Dean strolled up to stand alongside her. 'Neasden brings out the feminist in me,' he murmured. 'I foresee some spirited clashes between him and jolly Olly.'

Charlotte nodded. 'I like Vic and Olly very much. They'll keep the party lively. When you sat next to him on the plane, did you discover what the Professor's field is?'

'He's a political philosopher.'

'I'm not sure what that is. I know what philosophy is—the study of people's beliefs about God and human behaviour and the universe and so on. Presumably a political philosopher concentrates on the study of politics.'

'That's right, but I don't know much else about him.'

'But enough to know that you didn't want to share his cabin. When he stops reading to talk, is he a bore?'

'I don't know. We had very little conversation. Have you decided which bit of the deck you're going to spread your mattress on?'

'Probably here,' she said, indicating the space where they were standing. 'It wouldn't surprise me if, after the passengers have gone to bed, the crew fold up the deck chairs and sleep there, rather than below.'

'In that case, if you have no objection, I'll sleep on the other side of this boom.'

Beneath the boom was a large open-topped box for the storage of ropes. With various deck-lights to ventilate the forward cabins, it formed a barrier between one side of the deck and the other.

'Not in the least. If the roof of the saloon were flat, instead of being cambered, it would make a good place to sleep while the sea's calm.'

Suddenly, some way abeam, a school of dolphins began leaping out of the water in graceful arcs before, equally suddenly, they disappeared from view again.

'Not a bad life, this...sailing parties of tourists round the atoll,' said Dean. 'I wonder what the crew make of us? I was going to look at the names of their previous passengers in the drinks book, but the pages behind ours have been stuck together.'

Although Vic had written his surname, Parsons, in the book, Charlotte had put down her first name in case Manik looked at the book and recognised her surname as that of the old man his mother had worked for. As a child she had been called Pet by the islanders because that was what her grandfather had always called her. On the rare occasions when Manik had addressed her by name, he too had called her Pet.

An awareness of someone watching her made her turn her head and look straight into Manik's enigmatic golden eyes. He was holding one of the stainless steel shrouds supporting the masts, his other hand thrust into a pocket of his jeans.

'It's a beautiful evening,' she said to him. By now the sea had turned the colour of pewter, the sky to an apricot radiance.

He didn't come forward to join them, and for a moment she thought he was going to ignore her remark. His expression was far from friendly.

But after a slight pause, he said, 'Here is better than Europe, yes?'

'Much better,' Dean agreed. 'When we left Europe, snow was forecast.'

'I have read of snow but never seen it. I have visited other countries, but not where there is snow.'

Charlotte moved to perch on the rail near where he was standing. 'What countries have you been to?' she asked.

'Malaysia...Java...many places. Your dinner will be ready soon.' Barefoot now, he turned and moved silently aft.

The brief reply to her question, the walking away, were a snub that made Charlotte flush.

Had he recognised her? Was he angry because he thought she hadn't recognised him?

Already discomfited, she did not need Dean to say drily, 'A fairly clear indication that our skipper doesn't welcome blandishments from his female passengers.'

CHAPTER FOUR

'IT WASN'T intended as a blandishment. I was merely being friendly,' she said stiffly.

His left eyebrow lifted a fraction. 'You don't find him attractive? Most women would. You appeared to be admiring him earlier. But perhaps with a view to drawing him— I noticed the sketching equipment on your bunk. Are you an artist?'

'No, only a weekend sketcher. But you're right, the reason I was studying Manik earlier was that he has an interesting profile.'

'And you only flirt with Wasps . . . white Anglo-Saxon Protestants,' he added, in case she didn't know what he meant.

'I don't *flirt* with anyone,' said Charlotte. 'I usually try to make friends with people. Whether or not they're Wasps is a matter of indifference to me. I do know that Manik disapproves of our arrangement. He assumed that we were on holiday together. When he found out we weren't, he thought I should share with Diane or you with the Professor.'

'It's not his business,' said Dean. 'He's only responsible for our safety.'

'Perhaps he considers every aspect of his passengers' welfare is his responsibility.'

'If he mentions the matter again, you could point out that conditions on board aren't conducive to seduction,' Dean said drily. 'The bulkheads are far from soundproof, and even with a fan on the temperature between decks discourages close physical contact.'

Before she could answer, he added, 'Although perhaps he might not think so. These men are away from their own women for long stretches of time. It must add to their frustration to have tourist women running around next to naked.'

'They may not find foreigners attractive. White skins aren't particularly appetising in my opinion. Lobster-pink skins even less so. I think God made a great mistake in not making everyone toast-coloured.'

'I agree, but don't bank on our skipper not finding you attractive,' said Dean. 'In a few days' time you will be toast-coloured, and those brooding stares he keeps giving you may be an indication that he finds you very much to his taste.'

To Charlotte's annoyance, she found herself blushing, something she hardly ever did.

As she could not deny that Manik had been staring at her, or explain the probable reason for his scrutiny, she said, 'I'm sure he values his job too much to step out of line with any of the passengers.'

'He may find that some female passengers aren't averse to a holiday romance with a handsome yachtmaster.'

'He may, but I'm sure he's intelligent enough to know who's in the market for "romance" and who isn't,' said Charlotte.

Dean gave a slight shrug. 'Possibly. But it takes a clever man to read women's signals correctly. Isn't that right, Vic?' as the other man joined them.

'Isn't what right, mate?'

'I was saying to Charlotte that women's minds are hard to read.'

'Not half! I'll second that. I've been trying to read Olly's mind for twenty-six years and it's still a mystery. Unfathomable, that's the word for the female mind . . . totally unfathomable,' said Vic, with a teasing grin at Charlotte.

Somewhere amidships a bell rang, summoning them to supper. Everyone else had already taken their places at the trestle table which seated four on either side and two at each end.

The Professor was seated at one end with Olly and Sylvia Neasden on either side of him. Janet Warren was at the other end with Stanley Neasden on her left and a vacant chair on her right.

'You come and sit next to me, Dean. I can talk to Vic any time,' said Olly.

Dean took the chair between her and Diane and Vic the place next to Janet, leaving the space between Stanley and Bill for Charlotte.

'There: that's all the married couples split up and the men between the women, like a proper dinner party,' said Olly. 'If you'd had the end chair, Stanley, you'd have upset the balance.'

'Has my wife been bossing you around, Stan?' asked Vic.

'I prefer to be called by my full name, if you don't mind,' Mr Neasden said pompously.

'Right you are: Stanley it is. I can't remember anyone calling me Victor. I should think the last time was when I was christened,' said Vic.

Charlotte wondered what, if anything, would shake his imperturbable good humour.

As soon as they were all seated, the cook and his assistant served a large dish of fried fish with side dishes of potatoes and salad and a bowl of hot oil in which a great deal of finely sliced garlic had been fried.

The fish had been caught by the crew, using feather-baited lines, while they were sailing.

'Mm . . . this is delicious,' Bill murmured to Charlotte, after tasting a mouthful.

She noticed that Mr Neasden had no garlic on his plate and passed him the bowl.

'Not for me, thank you,' he said repressively.

'Garlic's good for you,' Olly told him from the opposite end of the table. 'Stops your arteries furring up or something.'

'If you don't have some, Stanley, you'll find the fumes from the rest of us unbearable,' added Janet. 'Do try it. It's very good.'

With marked reluctance, he took a very small helping.

While they were eating Bill talked mainly to Sylvia and Janet to Vic. On the other side of the table Diane was chatting vivaciously to Dean. After several abortive attempts to engage Stanley in small talk, Charlotte gave up trying.

As she concentrated on her food, she couldn't help overhearing the remarks of the cook and the steward who, hovering discreetly in the background, were making comments in their own tongue on the group round the table.

'These people don't eat as heartily as the German people we had before them, Hassan. The Germans had good appetites,' said the cook. 'The man with the face of a snake looks as if he had a plate of goat droppings in front of him.'

'Yes, but the girl beside him, she who swims under water, is enjoying it greatly, Ali. Look, she is taking some more,' said the steward. 'And the others are also eating well. It is only Snake-eyes who eats with a scowl on his face.'

The second course was tinned peaches, greeted with surprise and disappointment by the rest of the group, who had been expecting to enjoy an abundance of fresh tropical fruits.

Charlotte, who knew that on most of the islands fruit and greens had always been scarce and evidently still were, was glad she had brought some oranges with her. Only half a dozen, not enough to last the whole trip, but probably there would be days when the cook could get hold of a pineapple or some papaya.

Dinner ended with coffee. As none of them had had a full night's sleep on the plane, they were all beginning to feel tired and to think about turning in.

While the table was being cleared, Manik appeared.

'You have eaten well?' he asked.

'Very well, thank you, Skipper,' said Vic, leading the chorus of assent from which the only abstainer was Mr Neasden.

Manik gave a satisfied nod and went aft, where, in the shadows behind the wheel, washing up was in progress. Charlotte saw him light a cigarette, and presently the familiar scent, a compound of tobacco, honey and coconut, drifted towards her.

She had never smoked herself, except for a few experimental drags on other girls' cigarettes at boarding school, but when she was a child her grandfather had smoked through a hookah which cooled the smoke by drawing it through water. The fragrance of Manik's *bidi* evoked vivid memories of evenings on the veranda of the house her grandfather had built on the Kuda Thabu.

She was lost in a dream of the past when Mr Neasden stood up.

'Come along, Sylvia.' His unsmiling 'Goodnight' was addressed to the company in general.

The Professor being once more immersed in his book, Mrs Neasden had been talking across the table to Olly, although doing more listening than talking. But she jumped up at once and with a quiet, 'Goodnight, everyone,' followed him below.

'Like honeymooners, aren't they? Can't wait to be alone,' said Vic.

Diane giggled, but Olly frowned and said, 'Shush, Vic!' shooting an anxious glance at the others to see if they looked disapproving.

'I wouldn't mind stretching my legs on that beach,' said Bill Warren, turning to look at the island, now bathed in moonlight. 'But the noise of the boat coming back might disturb the Neasdens, and anyway, I think the crew are off duty now.'

The washing up had been finished and a low mellifluous murmur of Dhivehi and soft laughter came from the stern.

Charlotte rose. 'I'm going down to brush my teeth and organise my bedding,' she said to Dean.

'OK.' He half rose to his feet as she left the table.

It was her first visit to the washroom they were sharing. It had a small hand-basin built into a counter and a lavatory flushed by a pump. A notice giving instructions for using the pump, in German, Italian and English, was attached to the bulkhead behind it. Behind the basin was a mirror with recessed shelves on either side. Dean had already put his wet pack and a bottle of Autan insect repellent on the shelf on the right.

Charlotte put her toilet things on the left. Next to the galley was a large fridge where the cold drinks were stored. From it she had taken a bottle of water, but not for cleaning her teeth. For that she used tap water. Its brackish taste might worry Mr Neasden, and possibly some of the others, but it didn't bother her.

By the time she went back on deck everyone had dispersed except Dean and Diane.

'I'm not used to going to bed this early. He's teaching me to play Scrabble,' said Diane, looking up.

Rather him than me. I doubt if you can spell any words of more than one syllable, thought Charlotte—and then chided herself for being unkind and catty.

She had brought a small foot pump with her which made inflating the sun-bed very quick and easy. A few minutes later she was comfortably stretched out with her head on the pillow from her bunk and the myriad stars of the Equatorial night sky above her.

She remembered her grandfather telling her that when she looked at the stars she was looking back into the past; seeing them not as they were now but as they had been centuries ago, because the light from most of them had begun its journey long before his time and, from some of the distant stars, before the existence of man on the planet Earth.

The magic and mystery of the heavens was one of the many subjects he had discussed with her. Now, looking at the constellations whose names she had learned from him, she felt he was very close to her.

Something came between her and the moon; not a cloud but the shadow of a man.

'You may feel cold in the night. Here is a blanket,' said Manik.

Charlotte sat up. The sarong was tied to her waist now and her top half was covered by a cotton sweat-shirt.

'Thank you, Manik. I have a blanket I brought with me from Europe.' It was a vicuña blanket, very light but extremely warm, of the kind issued to First Class travellers on the airline Kay worked for. A careless passenger had burned a hole in it, which was how her friend had acquired it.

'But it was kind of you to offer it,' she added. 'I expect Dean Richmond would be glad to borrow it.'

'I will give it to him. He is with the woman with white hair.'

For a moment her mind slipped back to the time when they had been children together and she had corrected his first attempts to speak English. 'Blonde hair,' she said automatically.

'Blonde hair—thank you. I make many mistakes. I do not speak your language fluently. Goodnight.'

She knew by the tone of his voice that he was offended, but before she could tell him he spoke it extremely well he had gone.

She woke at first light and blinked in momentary surprise at the sight of the mast above her. Then she remembered where she was, and being rocked to sleep by the rhythmic motion of the boat.

In the night a breeze must have risen. Once or twice she had been aware of the wind strumming the rigging, but had never woken fully. Now she felt refreshed, eager to begin their first full day at sea.

Last night she had tucked a bikini under her pillow so that she could have a freshwater shower on deck soon after waking. Now, as there was no sign of anyone else being awake, and using the hose would be bound to be heard between decks, it seemed a better idea to swim over to the island, explore it, and have a shower when she came back.

No sound came from the other side of the hatches where Dean had intended to sleep. But, just in case he or anyone else suddenly appeared, she wriggled into the bikini under the cover of the blanket.

Her next action was to fold the blanket and the top sheet from her bunk which she had been lying on, and then to deflate the sunbed. When she uncapped the valve the air came out in a noisy rush which she feared might disturb Dean. But when she peeped over the boom which separated their sleeping areas, all that could be seen of him was the crown of his head and the long blanketed outline of his motionless body.

Making as little noise as possible, Charlotte climbed down the ladder and lowered herself into the water. At first it felt cold as she breast-stroked away from the schooner. But by the time she felt free to swim more vigorously, the sea had begun to feel warm.

She swam through the channel used by the dinghy the previous afternoon and soon was wading ashore on the kind of white crescent beach which delighted photographers supplying pictures for travel brochures.

Before she set out to circumnavigate the island, which she didn't expect to take her more than ten minutes, she paused for a moment to look back at *Sea Bird*. There were still no signs of life on board, and she wondered if the others had slept badly and now had fallen into the deep sleep which followed a restless night. She could imagine that the narrow bunks and confined space of the cabins would take some getting used to. Also the noise of the sea lapping against the hull would be louder between decks.

Feeling the need for some exercise after sitting around for nearly forty-eight hours, she did a few bends and stretches and then ran along the water's edge where the sand was firm. Now and then she did a ballet-leap to express the exuberance she felt at being in this lovely place at sunrise on a day when half the world, when they woke up, would be wrapping up against the cold.

After running the length of the beach several times, she slowed down and began to ramble along the shoreline.

It was just the same as it had been on Kuda Thabu. The fine powdered coral was criss-crossed with delicate lines like some intricate form of drawn thread embroidery on bleached linen. They were the tracks of the small, almost transparent crabs that lived in holes in the sand. As a child she had often tried to catch them, making them scuttle away, looking like small tangles of discarded sewing thread blown by the wind.

A stately reef heron, stalking through the shallows on long legs, watched her approach but delayed his take-off until she was only a few yards away.

On the other side of the island there was another beach, where she had another swim. She was sitting in the shallows, leaning back on her splayed hands and watching the incoming tide washing over her legs, when a quiet, 'Good morning,' made her nearly jump out of her skin.

'Oh…Manik…how you startled me! I thought I was alone.'

'I am sorry.' He was standing some distance away, wearing a pair of wet cut-offs, the early sunlight turning his smooth hairless chest to burnished bronze.

'It doesn't matter. Good morning. What a beautiful morning. Do you usually have a swim at this hour?'

He nodded. 'I saw you swimming while I was shaving. You are not afraid to come here by yourself?'

'What is there to be afraid of?' she smiled.

'People from Europe are sometimes afraid of snakes and spiders.'

It was a chance for her to tell him she had been to the island before and knew they were not infested with dangerous reptiles and insects. But she missed it. While she was hesitating, he said, 'Did you sleep well? You were not cold or uncomfortable?'

'I slept very well, thank you.'

'That is good. I don't think all did. At two o'clock I heard fan. Later, very loud snoring. I have read that this is a problem in Europe…not sleeping soundly?' As he spoke, Manik had come nearer.

'For many people, yes,' Charlotte agreed. 'In some ways life there is not as healthy as, for example, in the Maldives. In Europe people eat too much, drink too much, sit about too much.'

'But you are very healthy. I saw you running and jumping. Your body is in beautiful shape,' he said, looking at it.

Perhaps it was meant as a statement of fact, not a compliment, but his choice of words and the way his glance moved over her made her wonder if, in spite of her pale skin, he liked what he saw.

If Dean Richmond had made the same remark, she would have said thank you and tried not to blush. With Manik, she said, 'I am healthy... and I have the luck to enjoy my work, which many people do not.'

'What is your work?' he asked.

'I'm employed by a travel company to help tourists enjoy their holidays—but I'd rather you kept that to yourself. I don't want the others to know what I do for a living.'

'I will say nothing.'

'It's only because people in my job get big discounts on air fares that I can afford to come here,' she added. 'This is an expensive holiday which I expect the others have saved up for.'

He shrugged. 'I don't know what it costs. But I know that not many Maldivians are as rich as Europeans. To be rich is not important to me. I should like to have my own boat, but if that is impossible it doesn't matter as long as I am the skipper of a good boat.'

'Do you have a wife and children?' asked Charlotte.

He shook his head. 'The others have families. They work for nine months and go home for one month. That is not good. They are missing their women, their children very much.' His attention shifted to a point behind her. 'Someone is coming.'

It was Dean, strolling along by the water's edge as Charlotte had a short time earlier.

'I must go back to see that the preparations for your breakfast have started. Ali is good cook, but lazy in the morning,' said Manik.

He walked away in the opposite direction from the way the Englishman was coming.

'Good morning. You were up early,' said Dean, when he was within speaking distance of her.

'Oh, dear, did the noise made by my sun-bed deflating wake you?'

'No, I didn't hear you get up. Voices from below woke me. I saw you doing your daily dozen on the beach and then I saw him coming over——' with a nod at Manik's retreating back. 'It seemed a good idea to follow.'

She wasn't quite certain what he meant by that remark. Merely that a walk round the island had appealed to him? Or that the sight of the Maldivian following her to a place where she had disappeared out of sight and possibly out of earshot had made him uneasy?

'How did you sleep?' she asked.

'Pretty well. I was woken once or twice by the wind in the rigging, but I soon dropped off again.'

'Manik says he heard a fan buzzing during the night, and someone snoring. Had any of the others come on deck before you left?'

'Vic was up. He slept well . . . aided by a stiff slug of illicit whisky, I gather.'

'So he smuggled some in, despite Olly's scruples,' said Charlotte. 'I should think it was either the Professor or Mr Neasden who was snoring. Olly wouldn't put up with Vic snoring, but Sylvia seems too timid to object to anything.' She rose to her feet. 'I'm going back. I haven't got any sun-cream on and it won't be long before the day starts warming up. Also I'd like to have a freshwater shower before breakfast.'

'Me too,' said Dean. 'Tomorrow I'll have a cold-water shave on deck. Without any ventilation other than the door, the washroom makes me feel like a large turkey crammed into a small oven.'

'It is rather a hell-hole, isn't it? And worse for you than for me,' she agreed, as they started to follow Manik.

He was already back on board by the time the schooner came into view and they could see Vic hosing down Olly who, like Charlotte, was in a bikini. As they watched, Vic put his arm round her waist and gave her a playful kiss.

'Nice couple...Vic and Olly,' remarked Dean.

'Yes, and so are the Warrens. But I don't think the Neasdens or the Professor are much of an asset...at least, not if he's going to spend the whole trip with his nose in a book.'

'How do you feel about Diane?' Dean asked.

'When I saw her at Heathrow I thought her the arche-typal dumb blonde, but she may have hidden depths,' Charlotte told him.

'She can't spell, but neither could Churchill, so they say. I think she'll ask for her money back if there's nothing better than Scrabble on offer in the evenings. But perhaps some of the resort islands will have discos.'

'I'm sure they will. But whether the older members of the group will enjoy the sound of heavy-decibel pop is another matter.'

'As far as that goes, include me with the older members,' said Dean. 'Are you into reggae and heavy metal and so on?'

She shook her head. 'The only pop on the tape I made to bring with me is Elton John's *Blue Eyes*. The rest is what you might call "light classical"...Kiri te Kanawa singing opera, Menuhin playing violin concertos..that sort of stuff.'

'That's about my level too. Perhaps, later on, we can swop tapes.'

'Why not?' Charlotte said, smiling.

The appetising fragrance of toast and coffee was wafting from the galley when they climbed back on board.

She had brought a towel and a tube of shower gel on deck the night before, so she didn't have to go below before taking a quick shower. Her intention was to leave her hair in rats' tails during the day and shampoo it every evening.

After her shower, while Dean was taking his turn with the hose, she went below to change out of her wet bikini into shorts and a halter-top. Their cabin was immediately below the spot where he was washing himself and the water sounded like heavy rain drumming on the deck.

It seemed strange to open the wardrobe and find a man's shirts and jeans hanging alongside hers. Unlike her two flatmates, she had never lived with a man. Both Sally and Kay had had trial runs with men, but Charlotte, although she had twice thought she was in love, had never reached that stage.

There were some paperbacks on the upper bunk. She read their titles. One was a crime novel, two were travellers' tales and the fourth was an anthology of twentieth-century poetry, which rather surprised her. Dean had not struck her as a man who would bring poems on holiday with him.

He gave the impression of being cynical rather than idealistic, not a man with a soft centre. But what did she know about him yet? Very little. The confined space of the schooner forced them all to make friends more quickly than if they were staying at a hotel. Living in these conditions it was easy to forget they were a group of strangers who, at this time the day before yesterday, had not known of each other's existence.

Even Manik was a stranger now.

For breakfast, after a glass of sweet synthetic fruit juice, they each had a small, rather leathery omelette with toast and butter and pineapple jam.

Charlotte remembered the taste of tinned butter from childhood. She had often been grateful to her grandfather for bringing her up to eat whatever was put in front of her, so that now, unlike many of the tourists she dealt with, she was not fussed by being given unfamiliar or less than perfect food.

Predictably, several of the others agreed that the butter tasted like axle grease. In Mr Neasden's opinion it was uneatable. He complained that the toast was merely scorched, that the tea tasted unpleasant, that his omelette was overcooked.

Charlotte was wondering if she could endure two weeks of sitting next to him at meals when Dean said, 'Considering the size of the galley, and the heat when the burners are on, it's remarkable the food is as good as it is. I doubt if you'd do better, Neasden, if you were in charge of the catering.'

His tone had an edge which silenced any more carping and reminded Charlotte of her first impression on seeing Dean at Heathrow.

After breakfast they were taken ashore in the dinghy to spend the morning snorkelling.

'I expect the crew are glad to be rid of us and have *Sea Bird* to themselves for a couple of hours,' said Janet, as the dinghy returned to the schooner.

She and Charlotte began to walk along the beach, looking for a patch of shade in which to leave their gear while they were in the sea.

'What a night we had below deck!' Janet went on, with a grimace. 'You and Dean were in the best place. Would you believe that at two o'clock in the morning the Professor had his light *and* his fan on...and his cabin door open. Bill was furious, but I managed to restrain him from making a fuss. Then no sooner had the Professor gone back to sleep than Mr Neasden started snoring like a bull walrus. His poor wife! She couldn't possibly have slept through it.'

Charlotte said, 'Perhaps the Professor doesn't realise what a noise his fan makes in the small hours.'

'Perhaps not. Anyway, Bill's going to speak to him about it. What can be done about Stanley's snoring, I don't know. I shouldn't think Sylvia would dare to wake him and make him turn over. Perhaps she's used to the noise he makes and is able to sleep through it.'

The group had spread out along the back of the beach where palms and bushes gave shade. Before she went into the water, Charlotte intended to sunbathe for twenty minutes, then put on an old T-shirt to protect her shoulders and back while she was snorkelling.

She and Janet had applied sun-cream to each other's backs, and Charlotte was lying face-down with her head cradled on her arms, when there was a loud scream from somewhere not far away.

CHAPTER FIVE

LULLED by the warmth beating down on her, Charlotte did not react as fast as if she been sitting up.

By the time she had rolled over and jumped to her feet, Dean had sprinted past her, with Bill following him. Evidently the scream had come from the other side of a thicket of sea-grape.

When she and Janet followed the two men they found Diane, naked except for what was hardly more than a G-string, pointing to one of the bushes behind the spot she had chosen for her sunbathe.

'It gave me such a fright! I was oiling my legs and out of the corner of my eye I saw something move, and there it was...staring at me. Horrible, it was...ugh! I can't bear to think about it.' She gave a dramatic shudder, causing her sun-oiled breasts to quiver like chocolate-tipped blancmanges.

'What was it, Diane? A snake?' asked Janet.

'No, it wasn't a snake...it had legs. But it had a snake's nasty eyes and a long tail. I didn't like its expression. I'm sure it was ready to bite me. Ooh, I can't lie here, not with that thing in the bushes. I'll come round to where you are.'

As she bent to pick up her towel, the swing and bounce of Diane's spectacular bosom was a sight that held even the two women's gaze riveted.

'Whatever it was, I'd be surprised if it's aggressive,' said Bill. Charlotte saw him exchange an amused glance with his wife. 'According to the literature we were sent, the only potentially lethal creatures are the stonefish,' he added.

'I should think it was probably a large lizard,' said Janet.

'Whatever it was, I wasn't half glad when Dean scared it off,' said Diane, looking gratefully up at him.

He smiled at her. 'Any time, Diane.'

Charlotte turned away to go back to where she had been lying. To her chagrin, she found herself resenting Diane's unselfconscious display of her body. Could any virile man of Dean's age, on holiday without a partner, fail to be aroused by those lavish curves?

It was the first time Charlotte had ever felt jealous of another woman. She had always been happy with her own shape, even if it wasn't the kind to make men turn round for a second look.

However, although Dean might enjoy the sight of Diane spreadeagled on the sand not far from where he had put down his towel, it did not make him delay his snorkelling. By the time Charlotte had finished her short sunbathe, Dean, Bill and Vic were in the sea and the only men near were Stanley and the Professor who, as usual, was reading.

Charlotte suspected that from behind the screen of his dark glasses Stanley's eyes were feasting lubriciously on Diane's hot glistening flesh. But, if they were, Sylvia was too intent on her knitting to notice.

That evening the crew lit a barbecue fire on the beach.

The group aboard *Sea Bird* no longer had the island to themselves. During the afternoon another charter vessel had dropped anchor outside the reef and her passengers were also having a barbecue prepared for them not far from the fire Ali was supervising.

The people aboard *Thimara* were young Germans with whom, as they and the deep-water swimmers from *Sea*

Bird had their last swim of the day, Dean chatted in German.

Charlotte had often wished she could speak better German, but had found it easier to improve her command of the Latin languages rather than grapple with the complexities of the Teutonic tongues.

She wondered how Dean had come by his fluent German. Was it possible that he was an airline pilot? But although many continental pilots spoke several languages, none of the British pilots Kay had invited to their parties had been polyglots.

Later, when both groups had been taken ashore to eat, one of the men from the other group came over and spoke to Dean. Although her German wasn't good, Charlotte understood what he was saying.

'On your boat, they are mainly older people. Why don't you and the two girls come over and join us? There is plenty of food.'

'Thanks, but I think we should eat with our group,' said Dean. 'Perhaps I'll come over later.'

'With the girls! We have not enough girls,' said the German, his eyes on Diane. She was wearing a clinging jersey top without a bra, perhaps because she had stayed in the sun too long and her shoulders were sore.

'She doesn't speak German,' Dean told him.

'But I speak a little English...enough to chat up a girl with such fine boobs,' said the German, with a grin.

Charlotte glanced at Diane to see if she had caught the English slang words and realised he was talking about her. But the other girl was sipping a Coke, unaware of the young man's interest in her.

'In that case, why not ask her yourself...but not until we've finished eating,' Dean answered.

His tone had a slightly clipped edge which made the German nod and say a cheerful, 'OK, man,' before returning to his party.

Was Dean annoyed because the German was muscling in on territory he had marked out for himself? Charlotte wondered.

'Where did you learn your good German?' she asked.

'At school and on skiing holidays. Do you speak it?'

'A little...not enough to have interesting conversations.'

'I doubt if you'd find his conversation interesting,' he said, with a nod in the direction of the *Thimara* group. 'I would say his interests are food, beer and sex.'

She was tempted to say, 'What are yours?' but decided against it.

As they had the night before, Ali and Hassan watched the passengers from a distance while they were eating the barbecued fish and chicken. Manik, too, had come ashore but had gone for a walk along the beach.

When the hot food had been eaten, Hassan offered a large dish filled with what looked like small handfuls of sticky rice coloured bright crimson.

'It's not rice. I wonder what it is?' said Janet, when she and Charlotte had tasted the soft, sweet stuff, its flavour a compound of coconut and banana bound with some unknown substance. They had already discovered that neither the cook nor the steward spoke English.

'Manik will probably know,' Charlotte suggested.

'Let's go and ask him now...and get away from that music,' Janet added.

While they were eating, someone in the German party had turned on a transistor radio which was playing loud pop. The other group—none more than twenty-five and some of the girls much younger—were dancing.

'You may like that kind of music,' Janet went on, as they walked in the direction Manik had taken. 'I detest it...especially here. I don't think I should have liked it when I was young.' A few paces on, she added, 'And as I'm not young any more, it's really rather silly for me to want you to come with me to speak to the skipper. But I feel that if I were to approach him on my own— even at my age—he might wonder if I had designs on him. I'm sure these Maldivian men must think from the way we dress and behave that we have very loose morals.'

'Perhaps . . . I don't know,' said Charlotte.

The fact that she had grown up here did not give her any insight into the thoughts of Manik and his crew towards the Europeans and other foreigners they met. He was sitting on the trunk of a palm which had grown with its trunk curving low over the sand, smoking a *bidi* which he threw away as they approached. The coconut palms in the Maldives were unusual in yielding good wood for boat-building, and the kind of tree he was sitting on was particularly prized because its shape fitted the curve of a *dhoni*'s hull.

On Thabu, when Charlotte was small, the planking had been fixed in the old way, with wooden pegs, and the seams caulked with coconut fibre. She and Manik had spent many hours watching the boat-builders shaping the wood with their adzes and the skill inherited from their forefathers.

'I hope we're not disturbing you, Manik.' Janet explained what she wanted to know.

'The pudding is made from *agar agar* . . . a type of seaweed,' he told her.

'But is something added to it to make it that beautiful red colour?'

'I don't know. I will enquire for you.'

'Thank you—I should like to know. I enjoy cooking very much and like to take home some new dishes from the countries we visit. Thank you, Manik. We'll leave you in peace again.'

They had turned away to return to the part of the beach lit by the barbecue fires, when he said, in his own language, 'Have you forgotten we played together as children?'

Both women stopped and looked back; Janet because she had not understood what he said and Charlotte because she had.

In English, Manik said to her, 'We must speak together... alone.'

Aware that Janet was looking puzzled and uncertain, Charlotte said, 'It's all right, Janet. You go on, I'll follow presently.'

'Are you sure?'

Charlotte smiled reassuringly at her. 'I shan't be long.'

When Janet was out of earshot, Manik said, 'Why is she afraid for you? Does she think I will ravish you here, with many people near? The woman must be a fool.'

'There are parts of the world where women have reason to be afraid of men... some men,' said Charlotte. 'Mrs Warren doesn't know that you and I were friends long ago. Don't be angry with me, Manik. I thought you might not wish to be reminded of that time.'

'Or perhaps you hoped I would not remember,' he said brusquely.

'Why should I hope that? If you must know, it hurt my feelings when you didn't seem to recognise me...even though I've changed more than you have. I was only a child when we parted. You were almost a man.'

'Yes, you are greatly changed. You have grown into a beautiful woman. Many rich men must want to marry you.'

She laughed. 'If they do, they haven't mentioned it to me. I don't know any rich men and I've never had an offer of marriage. As I told you this morning, I work for my living. When did you know who I was?'

'From the first time I saw you. I knew you would come back one day. This is where you belong.'

He spoke as if it were a foregone conclusion; something predetermined long ago.

Before she could express her own uncertainty, he said, in Dhivehi, 'You had better go back to the fire. There will be other times when we can talk privately. Don't tell them you know me, and I shall say nothing to the crew. It is better so. Now be gone, girl.' The admonition was accompanied by a light push on her shoulder.

Disconcerted by this arbitrary dismissal, Charlotte did as she was told. But she walked back more slowly than she had come, her mind thrown into confusion by the discovery that he had known her identity all along and was not at all surprised by her return.

Did he really think her beautiful?

When she joined the others, Diane and Dean had left the *Sea Bird* party to join the other group.

'The rest of us are going back on board,' Bill told her. 'But you'll want to join in the dancing, I expect?'

'I don't feel like dancing tonight. I'll come back with you.'

It wasn't until they were back on board that Janet asked, 'Has Manik been chatting you up, as they say?'

'No, no...I—I corrected his English the other day. He's anxious to perfect it,' said Charlotte, hoping Janet would be satisfied with this impromptu circumvention of the real reason he had wanted to talk to her.

'Oh, I see.' Janet sounded relieved. 'I know he's very handsome and seems nice, but I don't think it would be wise to...to become too friendly with him. Not that you would, I'm sure. But Diane might have her head turned if he chatted her up.'

'Why wouldn't it be wise to be too friendly with him?' asked Charlotte, curious to know in what light Janet saw Manik.

The older woman looked uncomfortable. 'Well...he's an unknown quantity, isn't he? But perhaps that adds to his charm for a girl like Diane. I don't look at life the same way as your generation. I fell in love with Bill when I was young and he's been the only man in my life. Luckily he was the right man, and I don't feel I've missed anything. To tell you the truth, I shouldn't like being young today. I should never have had the courage to come on holiday on my own, like you two girls.'

'We aren't exactly girls,' said Charlotte. 'Anyone of eighteen would regard me as well over the hump! But you were talking about Diane and Manik,' she reminded her.

'I should think it's a long time since Diane was a virgin,' said Janet. 'She's probably had a lot of men and thinks she knows it all. But Manik belongs to another culture and sees everything differently. She might not be able to handle him as easily as the men back home.'

At this point they were joined by Olly and Sylvia, who had both been down to their cabins. Janet changed the subject.

Presently the three married couples agreed to play rummy. The Professor continued reading the book he had put aside before going ashore. And Charlotte fetched up her air-bed and prepared for another early night. But before she actually turned in, she spent some time sitting on the starboard rail, watching the activities ashore.

The fire built by *Sea Bird*'s crew had died down, but the other had been replenished and was burning brightly and the volume of the music must have been turned up. From where she was standing it sounded as loud as before, a raucous cacophony of noise from a culture far removed from this corner of a coral atoll where the natural sounds were the rustle of palm fronds and the soft swish of the sea.

Charlotte could see Diane dancing, but could not make out where Dean was until suddenly she saw him with one of the Germans, standing apart at the flickering fringe of the firelight, talking.

She peered at the spot where Manik had been sitting, but he did not appear to be there now. Perhaps he had walked further round the island to get away from the noise, which must sound even more discordant to his ears than to hers.

Presently she went to bed, and to shut out the blare of pop from the beach, put on her head-set and lay looking at the stars with the more soothing sound of Pavarotti's liquid tenor in her ears.

When she woke up, she knew by the colour of the sky that it was later than her waking time the day before. Too late for a solitary swim before breakfast. Already she could hear voices from the cabins. If she was going to have a shower before other people wanted to use it, she would have to be quick.

It was when she sat up and saw her cassette-player on the deck beside her, the wires to the head-set neatly coiled, that she realised she must have gone to sleep to the sound of Pavarotti singing.

Later, so gently that she had not been disturbed, someone had removed the head-set and switched off the player. Had it been Dean when he came to bed? Or Manik?

When she peered over the boom at Dean's sleeping space, neither he nor his bedding were there. Had he slept somewhere else? In their cabin? In Diane's cabin?

She was surprised at how painful the second possibility was to her. But from what she had seen of the way men behaved on holiday, she could not dismiss it.

If the beach party had gone on late, and most of the other people there were in pairs, it was likely there had been a good deal of heavy necking, and more, going on in the shadows as the fire died down. There might also have been smuggled hard liquor being passed around.

Diane was a sexy, seductive woman and no doubt, as Janet had suggested, an experienced one. Would Dean have refused what was on offer, either on the island or when they came back on board?

Possibly they had been brought back by *Thimara*'s dinghy, *Sea Bird*'s boat having come back earlier while the revelry was still going on.

She had just had her shower and was replacing the holder on its hook when Dean appeared, also dressed for swimming, and with water dripping from him.

'Good morning,' he said. 'If you've finished, I'll have a hose down.'

Charlotte moved away to dry herself. 'You're up early. I thought the party would go on until the small hours.'

'It did, but I left before the end.'

She couldn't help herself asking, 'And Diane?'

'She stayed, and the others dropped her off. I should think we shall have some complaints from Stanley at breakfast. There was a good deal of stage whispering and smothered giggling when she came on board, apart from the noise of the outboard motor. Diane may be feeling rather fragile today,' he added drily.

But clearly he wasn't, and Charlotte's mood swung from the irrational depression of a few minutes ago to its normal level.

'I went to sleep with my head-set playing and someone kindly took it off. Was it you?' she asked.

'Yes.'

'Thank you. I must be careful not to do that again.'

'What was it that lulled you to sleep?' he asked.

'A tape of that marvellous concert Pavarotti, Placido Domingo and José Carreras gave together in Italy a few years ago. Did you see it on TV?'

'I was lucky enough to see it live,' Dean told her. 'Some Italian friends pulled strings for tickets and invited me over.'

He must have very influential friends, she thought. 'Is that your world... music?' she asked.

It would have surprised her a little if he had said it was, and he didn't.

'Music is one of my pleasures, but as a listener, not a performer.'

He didn't go on to tell her what his world was, and she couldn't help feeling the oversight was deliberate. That, for some reason, he didn't want her or anyone else on board to know what he did for his living.

Could it be something disreputable like being a mercenary? He had the physique to be a commando and at times there was a hint of ruthlessness in the hard lines of his jaw and the set of his mouth. But was he the kind of man who would sell his military skills to whoever would pay for them?

The idea was as unacceptable as her earlier suppositions and, she hoped, as far from the truth.

'I'm going down to brush my teeth,' she said. 'I shan't be long.'

'There's no hurry.' Rough-towelling his hair, he smiled at her as she passed him.

Charlotte's heart did a strange little flip. What was it about this man which made her absurdly shy, as if she were nineteen again, a late developer, lagging behind her contemporaries in her relations with men?

A few moments later she came back.

'Someone's using our washroom. It may be the Professor. His cabin door was open and I don't think he was in it.'

Dean's displeasure at this information showed in his contracted brows and the sudden clenching of muscle at the angle his jaw.

'I wouldn't mind betting the old fool has broken the pump in his washroom. It will have to be mended—he's not sharing ours,' he said sharply. 'You wait here. I'll sort it out.'

Wrapping a towel round his lean hips and long-boned thighs, he disappeared forward.

Olly came on deck. 'What's up with Dean? He looks snappy this morning. Perhaps he's got a thick head? It wouldn't be surprising...the time they got back last night. Gone one o'clock it was. I heard Diane thumping about, but I didn't hear him. Did he wake you up?'

'It was only Diane who came back late,' Charlotte told her. 'Dean left the party earlier.'

'Oh...well, something's upset him,' said Olly. 'He brushed past me in the saloon with a scowl like a thundercloud. He did say "Good morning", but ever so brusque he was. Not like his usual self.' She cocked her head on one side, reminding Charlotte of a parrot. 'Have you two had words?'

'If Dean looks cross, it's because he thinks the Professor may have fouled up the pump in his washroom and be using ours,' Charlotte explained.

'I shouldn't be surprised. Have you noticed he's wearing the same shirt he wore on the plane? If he doesn't put on a clean one for breakfast this morning, I shan't be able to sit next to him. The pong puts me right off my food!'

'Perhaps at home he has a housekeeper who puts clean clothes out for him,' suggested Charlotte. 'He may put on whatever's to hand and not notice whether it's clean or not. Why not drop him a tactful hint, Olly?'

'I don't know a tactful way of telling someone they smell like a wino, love. Got any suggestions?'

'Morning, Charlotte. How're you today?' asked Vic, joining them.'

'Good morning. I'm fine, thanks. Are you?'

He nodded. 'But Dean's in a bate. You should hear him telling the Professor where he gets off! Not raising his voice or using strong language, nothing like that. But he's getting the message across that he's not pleased. I'll tell you something—whatever he does in the UK, he's not used to being answered back.'

'What was he saying to the Prof, Vic?' asked Olly.

Her husband put on an expression of extreme severity. '"It's bad enough for Miss Perivale to have to share her accommodation with me, Professor. It's quite intolerable that you should expect her to use a washroom left in this state...soap specks all over the mirror, the lavatory not properly flushed".' Reverting to his normal accent in place of the clipped imitation of Dean's voice, Vic said, 'My word, he was giving the old man a dressing down!'

'A good thing too,' Olly chipped in. 'Being brainy is no excuse for being scruffy, if you ask me. Especially in this hot weather, with us all cramped into a small space. Come on, Vic, let's have our showers before the others come up.'

Leaving them to it, Charlotte went aft. Vic's report of what Dean had said had kindled a warm feeling in her. She could not explain to herself why she should feel an inner glow because a man she scarcely knew found it intolerable that a washroom she used had been left in an untidy state. But it was so.

Presently Dean reappeared. 'The washroom's free. Sorry you've been kept waiting.'

'It doesn't matter,' she told him.

The washroom was now immaculate. As she stood in the small airless space, brushing her teeth, Charlotte thought about Vic's remark that whatever Dean did, he was used to authority. He was also accustomed to a high standard of cleanliness. Could he be a surgeon? That would explain why he wanted to avoid mentioning his occupation. Medical men usually were wary of revealing themselves for fear of having everyone's ailments inflicted on them.

As Dean had predicted, Stanley sat down to breakfast in a fume at being disturbed by the returning revellers.

Diane was still in her cabin, and when Olly went down to tap on her door and tell her the toast would be cold if she didn't hurry, the only response was a groan and a muffled instruction to go away.

The steward must have reported her absence to Manik who, when they had finished eating, stepped through the hatchway and asked, 'Is the blonde lady sick?'

'Not sick, Skipper. Tired from dancing,' Vic told him. 'And possibly other activities,' he added, under his breath, as Manik nodded and moved aft.

Unlike the Professor, he wore two clean shirts a day; a white T-shirt with *Sea Bird* printed across the chest in the morning, and a short-sleeved sports shirt after he and the crew had had their turn with the shower while the passengers were ashore.

Charlotte watched him take the cover off a hatch near the stern and swing himself into the hold housing the engine and generator. He was down there only a few minutes before reappearing, his biceps bulging under the smooth bronze skin as he hoisted himself back on deck. After wiping his hands on a rag, he came back to where they were lingering over their coffee and tea.

'Today we sail to Boduhithi, a resort island. It has shops and a bar, and tonight you can see traditional music and dancing. There is also a disco.'

Stanley rose to his feet. 'I have a complaint to make. Last night my wife and I were woken out of a sound sleep by the noise of people coming back from the island. I looked at my watch and it was exactly seventeen minutes past one. This shouldn't be allowed. It's your duty to stop it. If some people want to keep those hours, they should sleep on the beach . . . not disturb other people's rest.' He sat down.

Everyone looked at Manik, who gave a slight bow and said, 'I am sorry you and your wife were disturbed, sir. You are right: I am responsible for the passengers' safety and comfort. But each one of you has come to our country to enjoy a holiday, and, when some are old and some are young, this makes problems.'

His golden eyes swept round the table. 'I will speak to the younger people and request their consideration for those who wish to retire at an early hour. But I must also request the senior citizens to remember their young days and exercise tolerance.'

With another dignified bow, he turned away and began to give quiet instructions to the crew.

'He can't say fairer than that, Stanley, can he?' said Vic, as his wife began to stack the cups and saucers.

Charlotte had noticed that Olly, after years of mothering a large family, found it hard to sit still and be waited on. Looking after people was instinctive with her. Her nature was the antithesis of the Professor's pre-occupation with self.

Where had Manik learned the expression 'senior citizens'? Charlotte wondered. She had been impressed by his handling of Stanley's peevishness. But of course his maternal grandfather had been the *kateeb* of his island, and there might be the genes of leaders in the Scandinavian side of Manik's heritage. That his father had been a yachtsman, even if only a crew member, suggested that courage and self-reliance had been part of his make-up.

While the crew were taking down the awning and re-leasing the schooner from her moorings, Charlotte borrowed a bucket and, with the supply of washing powder she had brought with her, did her laundry.

'I'll have the bucket when you've finished with it,' said Dean, coming on deck with a bundle of clothes in his hand.

'You can use these soapsuds, if you like?' she suggested.

Olly, she guessed, would have offered to wash his stuff for him. But Charlotte thought men should be able to do their own chores and was curious to see what sort of job he made of it.

'Good idea. Thanks,' he said.

When she had finished squeezing the suds from her own clothes, he made a competent job of washing out his.

'That's women's work, sport,' Vic chaffed him, coming aft to get out of the way of the crew setting the sails.

'I don't have a woman,' said Dean. 'And if I did I wouldn't expect her to nanny me.'

'But she'd expect you to save her spoiling her nails if there was a tyre to be changed. If you ask me, the female sex is getting the best of this equality deal.' Vic gave Charlotte a wink to show he was only teasing.

The crew were hoisting the spanker, the schooner's mainsail. By the time Charlotte and Dean had pegged their washing to the wire guard rails aft of the saloon, *Sea Bird* had all her sails spread and the island was falling away astern.

'I hear you had a tête-à-tête with the skipper last night,' said Dean. The table and its trestles having been cleared away until the next meal, they were sitting in two of the green canvas directors' chairs, with *Sea Bird* stencilled on the back-rests, now spread around the after deck. 'Do you find him easy to talk to?'

Manik was now at the wheel, but he would not have heard Dean's question, for the schooner was about to change tack and all his attention was given to going about.

'Skippers, pilots, climbers, trekkers . . . all those kind of men are easy to talk to, don't you think?' said Charlotte.

'In the main, yes, I guess so. Was your father in one of those categories?'

'He was going to be an archaeologist, but I never knew him. He and my mother both died in a cholera epidemic in South America when I was a baby.'

'You weren't with them, presumably?'

'No, I was being looked after by my grandfather.'

'So his was the principal male influence while you were growing up.'

She nodded. 'Are you sure you aren't a psychologist? You seem very interested in influences?'

The question seemed to amuse him. 'Professional psychology is the last career I'd choose, but we all apply some psychology to our relationships with other people. Women are supposed to be heavily influenced by their fathers, or father-substitutes, so we're told.'

'And boys by their mothers,' she commented. 'Are you very close to your mother?'

'In the sense that we like each other—yes. But she's a painter and, as she specialises in painting people's gardens, now that my father is dead she's hardly ever at home. I have to catch her between commissions if I want to see her. Next month she's having an exhibition in London so we'll meet then, but even when she's not painting her diary is always full of engagements. She loved my father, but not to the extent that her life re-volved around him.' An affectionate smile softened the line of his mouth. 'She's not waiting for me to supply her with grandchildren.'

'What's her professional name?' Charlotte asked.

'Maris Richmond. Why not come to the private view of her exhibition and meet her?'

Before Charlotte could answer, he jumped up to offer a steadying hand to Diane who, flinching at the bright light, had just come on deck and was having trouble keeping her balance now the schooner was rolling gently.

'Hello, Diane. How are you feeling?'

'As if someone was boring a hole in the back of my head,' said Diane. 'It's impossible to sleep with all this racket going on.' She sank into the chair he had vacated and put on her mirror-lens sunglasses. 'Ah, that's a bit better.'

'I'll see if I can fix you a pick-me-up,' said Dean. He went below.

'Isn't that nice? He's a real gentleman, Dean. Not like that fella I was dancing with last night. There was only one thing on his mind, but he didn't get it, cheeky beggar. You came back early, Charlotte. Don't you like dancing?' queried Diane.

'Sometimes, but not last night.'

'Got your eye on him, have you?' Diane gave a nod at the helm, followed by groan at the pain caused by the incautious movement. 'I fancy him too, as a matter of fact, but I'll settle for Dean if you'd rather have Manik.'

'I wouldn't... I mean, I'm not out for a fling with either of them, Diane.'

'Oh, come off it! Don't be like that. You didn't come on your holiday to sit around talking to all these boring old husbands. Tell you what, why don't we toss for them? It's what fellas do when they see a couple of birds they fancy. Why shouldn't we do the same?'

It was difficult to find an answer that didn't sound priggish. While Charlotte was searching for one, Diane opened the handbag, which still went everywhere with her so that she could retouch her make-up, and produced a coin.

'You call. If your call comes up, you have first pick.'

At this Charlotte said firmly. 'No, Diane, I don't want to do that. It's not my style.'

The other girl shrugged. 'I don't see why not. Life is for living...that's my motto. We've got two good-lookers to choose from. I'm not going to spend my evenings playing rummy and ludo...not likely! To tell you the truth, I wouldn't mind having a fling, as you call it, with 'em both...and I bet you wouldn't either.'

When Charlotte didn't reply, Diane went on, 'If you don't fancy Manik, why were you up at the end of the beach with him last night?'

Whether by accident or design, her question came at the precise moment that Dean reappeared in the hatchway with a glass in his hand.

And to add to Charlotte's embarrassment, it was also heard by Manik, who had left the wheel in the hands of one of the crew while he went below. On hearing his name he had paused and now stood looking down at Charlotte, his expression inscrutable.

Conscious that both men were waiting to hear her reply, she found that all self-possession had suddenly deserted her.

It was Dean who ended the pause by saying, 'Here you are, Diane. Knock it back. It'll make you feel better.'

'What is it?' she asked, looking at the cloudy liquid.

'An antidote for hangovers.'

'Oh, well, I'll try anything once.' She drained the glass in two gulps.

'If it is convenient, I would like to speak to you...in the saloon,' said Manik.

'Who? Me?' Diane asked in surprise. 'Oh, yes...right you are...or should I say "Aye, aye"?' she giggled.

Manik gestured for her to precede him through the hatchway.

Dean sat down again next to Charlotte. Apart from the crew, all but one fishing from the stern, they still had this part of the deck to themselves. The others were all stretched out forward, sunbathing.

'I don't think Diane realises she's about to get a polite ticking off,' he said drily. And then, '*Do* you fancy Manik?'

CHAPTER SIX

'HE IS very good-looking,' Charlotte said. 'But my reactions to people are rather different from Diane's. I don't think looks are as important as things like kindness and humour.'

'But you would agree that it's physical attraction which starts a relationship?' asked Dean.

How could she deny it when, sitting beside her, his elbow inches from hers, was someone whose face and body—even the timbre of his voice—made her more sharply aware of her own body and of what she would feel if he touched her, caressed her, kissed her.

Trying to sound cool and detached, she said, 'Usually, yes. It would also be possible to start with a mental affinity, don't you think?'

'No, that comes later. You can't *see* mental affinities. You can see very early on that, if they were agreeable, you'd enjoy making love to someone. Haven't you ever felt that?'

'Hasn't everyone? But some people obey their impulses more freely than others. Diane says her motto is: life is for living. I go along with that...up to a point. But the quality of an experience is important. I can't imagine enjoying making love to someone if I didn't also find them interesting and amusing.'

'You expect a lot,' he said drily. 'An Adonis with brains and wit is quite a tall order.'

'I didn't specify that he had to be an Adonis...or a wit. Amusing was the wrong word. I meant that he'd have to share my sense of humour. The psychologists might be right: a girl *is* influenced by her father, or in my case her grandfather. Mine had the best sense of humour of anyone I've ever met. Sometimes, when he was reading me stories, or telling me stories about his life, we laughed till it hurt. I've never done that since he died.'

'When did that happen?' asked Dean.

Charlotte gave an involuntary sigh. 'A long time ago, when I was away at boarding school. After that I lived with another relation in the holidays. Sorry, I didn't mean to start telling you my life history.'

Manik reappeared and went to take over the wheel. But there was no sign of Diane.

'Perhaps he's upset her,' said Dean. 'It might be a good idea to go down and see if she's all right.'

Charlotte still had a suspicion that Diane might have embarrassed her deliberately. And she couldn't believe Manik's homily could have upset the other girl to the extent of making her retire to her cabin.

But she said, 'All right, if you think it's necessary.'

Before she tapped on the door of Diane's cabin, she could hear that the fan was on. The response to her knock was a shouted, 'Come in!'

Untidy was an understatement, thought Charlotte surveying the clothes-festooned cabin. For Diane's holiday wardrobe would not fit in the hanging cupboard. No doubt having learned from experience that the hangers provided were never enough, she had brought some with her, and these were hooked over the edge of the upper bunk from which her large suitcase projected.

'I know the place looks a mess, but what can I do?' she said. 'With nowhere to stand my case with the lid up, I can't find a bloody thing.'

'You've brought rather a lot for a sailing holiday. What did Manik want?' Charlotte asked.

'That'd be telling, wouldn't it?' said Diane, with a sly smile. Then she laughed. 'I'm only kidding. He's had a complaint from His Nibs about me waking him up when I came back last night, silly old twit. Manik was ever so nice about it. I could tell whose side he was on, but he has to put on a show if someone's complained, hasn't he? After he'd finished being serious, he gave me a smashing smile. I bet he's a different person when he's not being the skipper... when he can let his hair down.'

'Stanley made his complaint at breakfast in front of everyone,' said Charlotte. 'We guessed you were being ticked off and Dean thought you might be upset.'

'Did he? That was nice of him? Here, what d'you think of this?' Diane unhooked a hanger holding a red silk shift with sequined shoulder straps and thigh-high slits in the skirt.

'Very ooh-la-la!' said Charlotte 'Are you going to wear it tonight?'

'I might. What'll you wear?'

'I haven't bought anything glamorous.'

'You might be able to buy something on the next island. Manik says it's one of the high-class resorts—costs a bomb to stay there. You know what I said to you upstairs... on deck... about tossing a coin to decide which guy we'd have? I've been thinking that over. Do you know something?' Diane paused to hang the red shift in front of various other garments. 'I reckon if you'd agreed, and I'd won the toss and had first pick, I wouldn't have known which to choose. I mean, they're both smashing fellas, aren't they? While Manik was telling me off he was turning me on. So does Dean. When he looks at me with those steely grey eyes of his, I really flip. Don't you?'

The truthful answer was yes, but Charlotte said lightly, 'Wait till you see the Italian talent on this next island. Have you been to Italy, Diane?'

'No, never. Have you?'

Charlotte nodded. 'Italians are very good-looking, very romantic. Just hearing them speak turns me on. They sound as if they're making love when they're discussing the weather.'

'But we'll only be there for one night. We've got two weeks with Manik and Dean. Listen, I want to say sorry,' said Diane. 'It was rotten of me to put you on the spot about Manik. I could see you were ever so embarrassed. I won't do it again, I promise. I'm not like that usually. The fact is I was feeling lousy before Dean gave me that stuff to drink, and I thought you were putting me down.'

'Putting you down? Why should I want to do that?' Charlotte asked blankly.

'When you said in that toffee-nosed way, "It's not my style," I thought you were being superior. But I realised after that you weren't. You're different from me. You don't want to have a good time. You want to fall in love, don't you?'

'Yes . . . yes, I do. Don't you?'

'I don't believe all that stuff,' said Diane. 'My granny had to get married when she was eighteen, and my mum's had a rotten life too. One of my sisters is divorced and the other's not happy. So I've got my life worked out. A good-time girl, that's what I am. Until I'm getting near thirty. Then I'll look around for a guy who's a good provider. You can't have your cake and eat it in this life. You can't have a good time in bed with a hubby who never cheats. It doesn't work that way.'

'I disagree,' said Charlotte. 'My grandfather, who brought me up, was a terrible rake before he married my grandmother. But once he met her, he never looked at another woman. He didn't tell me—someone else did. I'm looking for a man like him.'

'You'll have a long wait, love,' said Diane. 'Phew! Even with the fan going, it's like a sauna in here. Let's get back on deck.'

Charlotte spent the rest of the morning reading one of the paperbacks she had bought at Heathrow. But she found it difficult to concentrate, and from time to time she gave up and lay back in her chair, looking up at the taut white sails.

Between the mainsail and the big triangular headsail secured to the schooner's bowsprit were two other sails, and *Sea Bird* was skimming over the deep blue ocean with a motion that reminded Charlotte of sitting in a rocking chair.

But when they had made their landfall and were anchored off Boduhithi, she was astonished to learn that Sylvia had spent the voyage lying in her bunk feeling seasick.

'Or it may be the food which is upsetting her stomach,' said Stanley, looking with disfavour at the big bowl of curried fish Hassan had set on the table for their lunch. The curry had been modified to suit European palates, and Charlotte found it too bland. But she guessed all the others, with the possible exception of Dean, would not have enjoyed a more fiery version.

After lunch they were taken ashore to swim from the beach.

'I think we should split up,' said Janet, as they stood in a group on the jetty. 'If we always go everywhere together, we could get a little tired of each other's company. Why not go our separate ways and reconvene at five when the dinghy comes back to fetch us?'

'A good idea, Janet,' said Olly. 'Come on, Vic. Let's head for the bar and have an iced G and T with a slice of lemon. If anyone else has the same idea, we'll pretend not to know you. *Ciao*, as they say here.'

The three married couples moved off, Sylvia looking pale and tired as she followed Stanley.

'I'm going to make a phone call,' said Dean. 'See you later.'

Diane and Charlotte watched his long purposeful stride in the direction of the public buildings.

'If he's making a call to the UK, it must be something important...or someone important,' said Diane. 'What's his job? Has he told you?'

Charlotte shook her head. She was equally curious. In spite of its remote situation, this nation of two thousand islands stretching across hundreds of miles of ocean had an up-to-date telephone system. But the cost of a call to Europe must be very expensive, and why would a man who had left London only three days ago need to make contact so soon?

'Let's go and look at the shops,' Diane suggested.

They found there was only one shop, but it had a good range of clothing and souvenirs, and clothes could be made to order for visitors staying on Boduhithi.

Diane wanted to buy a belt carved from turtleshell until Charlotte pointed out that it was against the law to import the shell into Britain.

While they were in the shop, an Italian tourist came in and looked admiringly at Diane. Hearing her speaking English to the assistant, he asked where they had come from. A few minutes later Charlotte drifted away to look at a rack of clothes all made from patchworked pieces of secondhand *batik* sarongs. The sun-faded patterns appealed to her, but she thought the price tags high and suspected she would be able to buy the same clothes for less in Malé, the capital, when they spent a day there.

Seeing that Diane and the Italian, who had introduced himself as Giorgio, were having a lively flirtation, she left them to get on with it and went in search of a quiet stretch of beach.

She was lying in the shade of a sea-grape when suddenly Dean loomed over her.

'Are you enjoying your seclusion, or may I join you?' he asked.

'Of course. Did you get through all right?'

'Yes, thanks. No problem. Where's Diane?'

'I left her in the shop, being chatted up by Giorgio from Milano,' Charlotte told him.

'What do you think of this island? Have you looked around?'

'Not exhaustively. I like the general layout...the wide cedar decking walkways have weathered to a lovely grey, and it was a good idea to plant an avenue of palm trees as the main axis.'

'The Italians are a nation of artists. Their projects always have style. Because they were enthusiastic divers before the sport caught on elsewhere, they were the first Europeans to see the touristic potential of these islands. I'm told the Italian charter boat, the glamorised *dhoni* called *Fathuhul Bari*, is a cut above most of the charter boats. We may run across her somewhere.'

Charlotte was lying with one hand cupped under her head and the other one idly sifting the powdery coral.

Dean, leaning on one elbow beside her, began to do the same thing. 'Do you know how this stuff is made?' he asked.

She did, but she said, 'Tell me.'

'It's been processed by parrot fish. Coral lives on plankton and parrot fish feed on the algae in the reef. They have strong jaws to break off and munch the hard limestone protecting the coral, and this is the waste from their meals. How much sand do you think one parrot fish can produce in a year?'

She remembered being asked the same question by her grandfather, long ago. Unlike the facts pumped into her at school and later forgotten, most of the things she had learned from him had stuck.

Trying to look thoughtful, she said, 'It depends, I suppose, on the size of the parrot fish. Ten pounds?'

'One tonne a year.'

She widened her eyes. 'You're joking!'

'So are you, naughty girl. You knew all the time.'

'Yes,' she admitted. 'But it is a fascinating fact that if it weren't for the parrot fish these islands wouldn't exist.'

She stretched, closed her eyes and gave a sigh of pleasure. 'How lucky we are to be here...away from the winter for two glorious golden weeks!'

'That's a gloriously golden tan you're working up,' said Dean.

There was a note in his voice that made her open her eyes. She was just in time to see him lean closer, his eyelids closing as he swooped down to kiss her.

There was an interval in which her heart seemed to stop beating as his lips touched hers, lightly at first and then with the practised assurance of a man who had kissed many women and knew how it should be done.

It was a kiss which Charlotte felt to the tips of her fingers and the ends of her toes; an explosion of sensual delight that permeated every nerve and cell of her body. Partly because she had not been kissed for a long time. Mostly because of the chemistry which had been building up since she first saw him.

He drew back a little to look down at her.

'Nice?' he asked.

He was confident that her answer would be affirmative, and Charlotte didn't dissemble. She had never seen the point of being coy.

'An understatement,' she murmured.

'Let's do it again, then.'

As their lips touched for the second time, she felt her insides clench with mounting excitement. It was just as well it was daylight and they were on a public beach. Already he made her feel that, if they had been somewhere private, these first soft exploratory kisses could have only one outcome.

But if Dean felt the same way, as she was sure he did, being male, with a male's rapid boiling point, he didn't hurry the process. Perhaps he was also aware that they were in a place which put a limit on how far he could go. Or perhaps he was too sophisticated and experienced ever to rush these delicious preliminaries.

They had been kissing for some time before he drew back and said, 'This could get out of hand. I'm going to have to go and cool off in the sea.'

In a single lithe movement he was on his feet. Charlotte watched him walk down the beach and enter the colourless water of the shallows, knowing that it must have taken considerable will-power for him to break their embrace. A moment ago those powerful shoulders had been bent over her. She had felt the shift and play of the muscles under the smooth olive skin which already was well on the way to a deep even tan.

What is this he ... we have started? A holiday affair or something more serious? she wondered. I could have stopped it after the first kiss. He gave me a chance to give him a diplomatic brush-off, but I didn't take it. Because I want him. But do I want him because life is for living, especially on holiday? Or do I want him for the rest of my life?

A few minutes later she stood up and ran down the beach to join him in the sea. She needed to cool off too, even if her body didn't signal her emotions as clearly as his did.

From other beautiful beaches in the various parts of the world her job had taken her to, she had watched people in the water kissing and caressing, sometimes to an extent which had made her embarrassed for them. Making love was or should be a private pleasure; not something to be done furtively in front of onlookers. Although she longed to feel Dean's hands on her body, she hoped he wouldn't touch her now.

He didn't. Although the only people in sight were some distance away, he behaved as if their kisses under the sea-grape had never happened and they were just two fellow passengers having a leisurely swim together.

Charlotte wondered when he would kiss her again. Perhaps tonight when they came ashore again for the concert. It seemed a long time to wait.

For dinner that night Diane put on her red dress. She hadn't spent all her time ashore with Giorgio. She had found that the island boasted some 'very swish' public washrooms tiled in navy blue and supplied with fresh water.

'So I washed my hair in one of those guitar-shaped things like a mini jacuzzi.'

'A bidet?' said Charlotte, to whom she confided this enterprising act.

'That's right... a bidet. I know what they're really for. But it was clean, so why not?' Diane ran her fingers through her mane of blonde curls and ringlets. 'It feels lovely and clean. I styled it with my new combi-tong-brush.' She glanced at Charlotte's straight hair. 'I'd lend it to you, but I've only got the one gas cartridge. You're not allowed to take spares on an aeroplane.'

'It's a kind thought, Diane, but actually curls don't suit me.'

Charlotte was wearing a pair of white cotton shorts, cuffed just above her knees, with a navy-and-white striped French top with a boat neck and cap sleeves. Navy rope-soled espadrilles and a navy scarf slotted through the loops of her shorts completed her outfit, which she had accessorised with a couple of red plastic bangles and large red button ear-rings.

'Still, you look very nice,' said Diane, although it was clear she considered Charlotte's outfit rather low-key for an evening on one of the smart islands.

Janet was equally informal in a simple printed cotton sun-dress with a triangle of matching cotton to cover her shoulders if a breeze should spring up.

The next to appear was Olly, in a loose pink dress with pleats falling from a crocheted yoke. Charlotte guessed and Olly confirmed that it had been bought on a previous holiday on one of the Greek islands.

Finally Sylvia came on deck in a floral dress clearly made of some mixture of synthetic fibres which would be uncomfortably hot in a tropical climate. Obviously she had no idea what was appropriate on a sailing holiday, Charlotte thought sympathetically. Her sandals had small sharp heels which would leave marks on the deck. Her necklace of coloured paste didn't go with the colours of her dress and her watch was a marcasite cocktail watch, with a tiny face, which might have been bought for her mother in the Thirties and wasn't right for the Nineties except perhaps worn with two or three other period pieces on the wrist of a girl of eighteen.

Sylvia was the kind of woman who made Charlotte long to be able to take her in hand and bring out her good points. Not that Stanley would be likely to appreciate his wife's transformation.

For dinner they had three large pizzas made by the island's chef and accompanied by a more interesting salad than any they had had so far.

At Olly's suggestion, all the men had changed places, and now Dean was opposite Charlotte and she was no longer next to the group's biggest bore but between the Professor and Vic.

Dean had put on a pair of well-cut grey linen pants and one of the nicest T-shirts she had ever seen; blue-grey cotton with some navy lines across the chest representing the sea and several leaping and diving dolphins. On one side of this design was written, in small letters, *Martha's Vineyard*.

Leaning towards him, she said, 'I've always wanted to visit Martha's Vineyard and Nantucket. Have you been to both islands?'

'Only to the Vineyard. I have friends in New York who have a weekend place there.'

'Must be rich people, your mates,' said Vic, who had been listening in.

'There are rich people there,' Dean agreed. 'But it's not an exclusive place. Some people have modest incomes and simple tastes. My friends have a fisherman's cottage they've renovated themselves.'

'It seems wrong having pizza without wine. Don't you think so, Janet?' said Olly.

The conversation ebbed and flowed, and sometimes Charlotte joined in and sometimes she was silent, preoccupied with the question of where this afternoon's kisses would lead, and whether, like countless girls and women before her, she was allowing a romantic setting and unsatisfied longings to cloud her judgment.

She had not reached her present age without knowing that, although she didn't look as sexy as Diane, she had a passionate nature which had never found its full expression. And the longer she had to repress all those innermost feelings, the more violently they would erupt when they were released.

Her instantaneous response to Dean's first kiss had proved that it wouldn't take much to break down her inhibitions. A stroll in the moonlight...an empty beach...a secluded place in the shadows...the sensuous scent of Arabian jasmine...more kisses...she could be swept away by undercurrents as powerful and potentially disastrous as those in the ocean.

Since a nasty fright during her childhood, she had never taken risks with the sea's power. Was it a folly she would later regret to take chances with a man she found compellingly attractive but didn't really love?

And what about Manik, to whom she was also attracted and with whom she had much closer links?

CHAPTER SEVEN

THE concert of traditional Maldivian music began with *bodu beru*, meaning 'big drum.'

Charlotte had heard her grandfather tell of the wild dances performed by men who, in the frenzied climax of a dance called the *tara*, had stabbed their heads with knives until the macabre ritual had been banned by the government. She herself, as a little girl, had imitated the rhythmic swaying of the *bandiya jehun* danced by women.

Tonight, elaborated for the benefit of the tourists, it was performed by a team of girls whose long hair looked like thick skeins of black silk. They were wearing the *dhivehi libas*, a long-sleeved silk dress with many narrow bands of embroidery forming a collar. Kneeling on mats, the girls tapped the rings on their fingers against the sides of metal pots.

The concert included some love songs whose tunes were more congenial to European ears than the *raivaru* folk song which Charlotte could see was not being enjoyed by the others in the *Sea Bird* party.

They were seated together in one of the rows of cane chairs in the island's open-sided auditorium. As she glanced along the line of faces to gauge their reactions, she saw Manik, his arms folded, leaning against one of the pillars supporting the roof of the building.

But instead of looking at the stage, he was watching her. She smiled at him, a little surprised that he should be present at a performance he must have seen many times. Had he been intent on the stage, she would have

111

wondered if he were interested in one of the girls, all of whom were exceptionally pretty with long lashes and ravishing smiles.

Manik acknowledged her smile with a slight inclination of the head. He was looking very spruce in white trousers and a black shirt. As a boy he had always worn a *lungi*, a length of checked cotton wrapped round the lower half of the body like the sarong of South-East Asia. But perhaps now the *lungi* did not accord with his status as a qualified sea captain.

When, a little later, Charlotte glanced in his direction again, it was disconcerting to find his gaze was still fixed on her. Looking away, she continued to feel herself the cynosure of that enigmatic scrutiny. Perhaps he was staring only because he found it difficult to relate the woman she had become to the child he had known.

The concert was nearly over when one of the island staff came and whispered in Dean's ear. Watching his discreet departure, Charlotte concluded that he had been called to the telephone to speak to the person he had rung earlier.

He was still absent when the performance came to an end and she and the others made their way to the bar. At least, that was where she was heading until a light touch on her arm made her turn to find Manik beside her.

'I must talk to you,' he said quietly, in English.

She was bringing up the rear of the group and knew that, if she was missing when they got to the bar, they would think she had slipped away to the place where Diane had washed her hair.

'It's a long time since I heard music like that,' she said, as they turned down the walkway that led across the beach to a long palm-thatched pier built over the lagoon.

The pier was not a private place; anyone sitting or strolling there could be seen in silhouette from the island. At the moment it was deserted.

Manik said, 'I came to find you this afternoon. I thought you would be in the sea, but you were not swimming. You were lying on the beach with Richmond. You were kissing.'

The last time Charlotte had felt guilty had been when a mistress at school had caught her performing a 'dare' halfway up an ancient wistaria creeper which the girls were forbidden to climb. She had thought she would be expelled and her heart had lurched in the same way as it did now, even though this time she had done nothing wrong.

'Perhaps I have not understood correctly,' said Manik. 'I thought you and Richmond were not knowing each other before the plane brought you to Malé.'

'We were not,' she agreed, wondering how long he had stayed to watch their embrace.

'Your grandfather would not be pleased.'

'I'm no longer a child. I'm a woman now, Manik. My grandfather would have kept his thoughts to himself.'

'Are you telling me I should not speak on this matter?' he asked stiffly.

'I don't think being the captain of *Sea Bird* gives you the right to tell me how I should behave. I'm not a young girl in need of advice and protection!'

'Any woman for whom men hunger need Once I was like a brother to you. Will you right to warn you when you are behavi know Europeans do not live as we do. the tourist women bare their breasts, men drink until they cannot walk str are bad. Ours are better.'

'Oh, do stop preaching!' she ex as well as I do that Maldivian wo their breasts bare before Muslim customs prevailed. The divorce rate here is as high as it is Europe, possibly higher. There were people on Thabu who'd been divorced six or seven times. And although alcohol is forbidden, *raa*, if it's left to ferment, becomes alcoholic. Human nature is pretty much the same the world over, so I don't want to hear a lecture about the immoral behaviour of Europeans compared with the saintliness of the islanders!'

'You are angry because you know you are in the wrong...that you should not have let Richmond kiss you.'

Manik spoke in his usual quiet voice. But instinct told her it was he who was angry. And when Manik lost his temper...watch out! Or that was how it had been when they were children.

The Maldivians were not, as a race, people who vented their feelings in quarrels and fights. But Manik was part-Norwegian and, as a boy, had been capable of aggression, given enough provocation. Charlotte had once seen him punch another boy who had been disrespectful to Alima, Manik's mother.

But that was a long time ago, and now that he was a man he might have mastered the hot temper inherited from his Norse ancestors.

'You're being old-fashioned,' she said. 'I'm sure you've kissed plenty of girls. Why is it wrong for me to let a man I like kiss me?'

'Because the next time you are alone with him, he will ᴉnk he can do other things...touch your breasts and...I ot know a polite word for what he will try to do to

olite term is "to make love",' she told him. clined his head. 'Thank you.'

ity, when she felt sure he was longing to e had once or twice when they were children, appealed to Charlotte's sense of humour, never far below the surface. She couldn't help laughing.

The next thing she knew was that Manik had grabbed her by the shoulders—but not to shake her. To her astonishment, his next action was to kiss her.

It was very different from Dean's first kiss. Manik's kiss was like a squall hitting a small boat, catching the helmsman unawares. But, unlike a squall, it didn't last long. She was momentarily rocked off her feet and would have lost her balance if he hadn't been holding her. But almost before she had time to register the bruising pressure of his mouth on hers, it was over.

For a few seconds longer he kept the painful grip on her shoulders as he looked down into her face, his golden eyes narrowed to fierce slits. Then he released her and stepped back.

Without a word, he turned and walked away.

Charlotte remained where she was, rooted to the spot by amazement and a variety of conflicting emotions she knew it would take some time to disentangle.

But one thing was clear and deeply disturbing. Manik's kiss had not left her cold. In a different way, it had been as stirring as Dean's.

I can't fall in love with them both, she thought, aghast.

Yet there was no getting away from the fact that today, within a few hours of each other, two tall, dark but otherwise completely dissimilar men had excited her with their kisses. She would not have believed it was possible. But it had happened. Her heart was still drumming from being held by Manik, and only this afternoon it had beat faster in Dean's arms.

She was remembering the interlude on the beach on the other side of the island, when she saw Dean himself coming towards her along the walkway.

Had he seen Manik kiss her? Had the others? She could see them clearly enough, sitting in a group of chairs under the whirling ceiling fans in the large well-appointed lounge-bar. But she hoped they were too busy enjoying their drinks and chatting to have noticed the incident on the pier or, if they had, to have recognised the silhouettes of the participants.

She would soon find out if Dean *had* seen, she thought apprehensively, as he came towards her. Even if he were only amusing himself with her, he wouldn't like another man poaching on territory he considered his, at least for the duration of the cruise.

'All alone?' he asked, as he joined her.

As it didn't seem like him to state the obvious, she wondered if he was being satirical. Even if he had not seen the kiss, she felt sure he must have seen Manik striding away from the pier.

She decided the best reply was, 'You've been telephoning, I presume? Has anything world-shaking happened since our departure?'

'If it has, it wasn't mentioned. What about a cappuccino, or something stronger?'

His tone being casual, Charlotte relaxed. Clearly he hadn't seen the kiss.

'I'd enjoy a cappuccino.'

They strolled back to the beach, their shadows moving ahead of them on the cedar planking, the outline of Dean's tall figure stretching a yard beyond hers.

When they arrived at the bar, as all the chairs were taken where the others were sitting, Dean took her lightly by the elbow and steered her to two empty chairs some way from the English group.

Most of the Italians in the bar were wearing expensive and elegant resort clothes and many of the girls had wonderful tans and a glamour which made Diane's red outfit look cheap and showy.

As she remembered he had named Italy as one of his favourite European countries, and thinking it likely that he spoke Italian, it occurred to Charlotte that Dean could have spent a pleasant evening here had he arrived on his own. Judging by the approving stares he was attracting, he would not have been alone for long.

Manik too would have no problem picking up a companion, if he wanted one; and she wouldn't mind betting he had sometimes made the most of his opportunities. What seafarer didn't? Particularly if he was single.

She supposed she ought to be flattered that two personable men had both chosen to focus their attention on her, and in a way she was, for she knew she couldn't hold a candle to some of these lovely Italian creatures in their early twenties.

At the same time she found her situation unnerving. For several years she had felt that the cataclysmic love she had dreamed about when she was younger was never going to materialise and that sooner or later she would have to settle for a more pedestrian relationship.

Now, all at once, she had the most compelling man in sight fetching coffee for her, and another man furiously angry with her. And not only angry. In the second before Manik had let go of her, she had felt his involuntary reaction to kissing her. He had gone, but he had wanted to stay; to do all those blissful things for which, until she had told him, he had not known the polite words.

'Cappuccinos coming up, and I ordered a couple of Camparis with soda as chasers. Is that all right, or do you hate the stuff?'

'I like it,' said Charlotte.

She was remembering how, at the beginning of her career, she had seen an innocent tourist from the Midlands become legless after drinking several Camparis under the impression that anything pink in a tall glass was non-alcoholic. Surely Dean couldn't think she was equally naïve? Couldn't have it in mind to try the classic method of loosening a girl's inhibitions before suggesting a stroll in the moonlight?

She didn't want to believe it of him, but she had spent the past six years watching people on holiday let wishful thinking prevail over common sense. Manik too must have seen numerous female tourists allowing themselves to be sweet-talked by men who would wave goodbye and forget them at the end of the voyage. Maybe she shouldn't dismiss Manik's warning out of hand. Perhaps his assessment of Dean was sounder than hers.

As a waiter brought Dean's order to them, there was a public announcement that the disco was starting. It wasn't long before more than half the people there had gone to dance.

'Are you in a dancing mood tonight?' asked Dean.

'Not really. Are you?'

He said, 'I like to dance at close quarters with my partner, but I should think it will be an hour or two before they get around to playing that sort of music. Like you, I don't find this climate conducive to vigorous exercise, apart from swimming.'

An Italian, whose chair was back to back with Dean's, turned round and asked if they were staying on the island. He was some years older than Dean and the woman with him was his wife, but she did not speak English. When it emerged that both Dean and Charlotte spoke Italian, a four-way conversation in that language began.

They were still chatting half an hour later when Charlotte noticed that the Warrens and the Parsons were leaving. Stanley and Sylvia had been at the concert, but she had not seen them, or the Professor, in the bar. Diane, of course, had joined the exodus to the disco.

'Our lot are on the move, Dean. Perhaps we ought to go too,' she suggested.

'But the night is young,' said Luciano, in English. 'I would like to buy you a drink. Surely you need not return to your yacht at this early hour?'

'You're not tired, are you, Charlotte?' asked Dean.

'No, I'm not tired, but Maumoon may be...our boatman,' she added, in case he hadn't yet mastered the crew's names. 'Maldivians are larks, not owls.'

'I'll dash him some *rufiya*,' he said easily. 'He won't mind staying up late if he gets something for his piggy-bank.'

This was undoubtedly true, and Charlotte was happy to continue talking to Luciano and Clara, especially as he was the owner of a travel agency in Milan and had some interesting views on the future of tourism. Clara was also in business, with two dress shops, one in Milan and one in Florence. And as Charlotte loved clothes, although she would never be able to afford even the ready-to-wear models of her favourite Italian designers, Valentino and Armani, she was able to discuss their influence on clothes at chain-store level.

Had they been staying on Boduhithi, they might have continued talking to the Italian couple until midnight or even later. But shortly before eleven Diane reappeared.

'That Giorgio's a proper devil!' she giggled. 'He's trying to get me to stay the night in his bungalow. He's lying in wait for me near the jetty. I'll have to come back with you two.'

Charlotte was rather relieved by this turn of events as, much as she had been enjoying the Italians' company, she did not like keeping Maumoon up long past his pre-ferred bedtime. If Giorgio had been intending to waylay Diane, the sight of her tall escort must have given him second thoughts.

But it was not Maumoon who was waiting in the dinghy when they arrived at the jetty. It was Manik.

'Hello, Skip. What are you doing here?' Diane asked chirpily. She had had a good deal to drink and had clung to Dean's arm to steady her on the way from the bar to the jetty. But she had not had enough to make her succumb to Giorgio's lures.

'I am waiting for you and the others, Miss Baker,' he said, helping her into the dinghy.

'You should have come to the disco. I bet you're a smashing dancer!'

Manik ignored this remark. As soon as she was seated, he offered his hand to Charlotte.

Instead of taking it, she rested her fingers lightly and briefly on his bronzed forearm as she stepped into the boat and sat down next to Diane. Then Dean, unaided, stepped inboard and Manik untied the painter, pushed off and started the engine.

The expertise with which he cut the motor some way from the schooner, so that the dinghy's momentum was precisely enough to make it glide alongside with a minimum of disturbance to those who might be asleep, was probably lost on Diane. But Dean must have recognised it, and certainly Charlotte did.

However, although the Neasdens had turned in, Vic and Olly and the Warrens were still on deck, playing cards. But there was no one in the saloon. The crew had gone to bed.

'Hello, Diane, you're back early. I thought you and that sexy Eytie you picked up would be dancing till dawn,' said Vic, in mock surprise.

Charlotte went below to change and brush her teeth. When she climbed up the companion ladder with her bedding under her arm, Manik was in the saloon, sitting on one of the banquettes. Their eyes met and she thought he might say something, perhaps apologise. But the saloon was only three steps down from deck level, and it could have been the proximity of the others which kept him silent.

'Goodnight,' she said, in a low voice.

He did not answer.

She slept badly, troubled by vivid dreams of the past.

In the last dream, which woke her up in the early hours and left her unable to sleep again, she and Manik were children, listening to her grandfather telling them about the Vikings, the ancestors of the father whom Manik had never known.

Lying awake, waiting for dawn, she realised that her grandfather had told those stories—how the Vikings had traded with the great city of Constantinople and provided the imperial guard there—to boost Manik's self-esteem.

It was her grandfather who had arranged for the boy to go to sea under the wing of the Norwegian master of a freighter bringing supplies from Singapore to Dhivehi Raffe, 'the island nation', as it was known to its inhabitants.

But for the old Englishman's intervention, the best Manik could have hoped for was a place on a fishing boat. Fishermen, unless they were boat-owners, made a precarious living. Most of the catch went to the owner, the remainder being shared by half a dozen crew. When catches were poor, they and their families barely had enough to eat.

In those days tourism had been in its infancy. Now that the Maldives were a popular holiday destination, with an increasing number of islands being made into resorts, young men from the poorest communities could seek a living elsewhere. But it meant separation from their families.

Manik, after his mother's death, had had no family other than Charlotte's grandfather and herself. He was used to being alone.

She wondered why, if he had wanted to kiss her, he had done it only once. Perhaps he had thought that if her head was being turned by Dean she would be bound to dislike being kissed by another man. And perhaps he was right to think that a normal reaction.

Yet how, when they had been so close as children, could she ever be afraid of or repelled by him?

How many times, when she was little, had he picked her up and dusted her down after a tumble? How many times, later on, had he tended the cuts and coral-grazes she had inflicted on herself? Once, if he hadn't been there, she might have drowned.

Between them, her grandfather and Manik had shaped her conception of what men and boys were like...strong, brave, protective, impatient but never unkind. It was only later, in England, that she had discovered some of the male sex fell short of the standard set by her two mentors.

Having been awake, so it seemed, half the night, when the sky was beginning to lighten she fell into a heavy sleep, from which she was woken by someone's hand on her shoulder.

She opened her eyes to find Dean bending over her.

'Time to get up if you don't want to miss breakfast.'

Blinking, confused, Charlotte struggled into a sitting position, her first clear thought being that she must look a mess—heavy-eyed, hair in a tangle.

'Thanks...I'll be right there.'

She felt better after a quick dip over the side, followed by five minutes with a toothbrush and comb in the washroom. It was stuffy down there between decks. She was glad to get back in the fresh air, wearing her sarong, her hair towel-dried and sleeked back from her face.

To her surprise, Janet said, 'You slept well by the look of you, Charlotte. What it is to be young! I had a dreadful night and I feel like Mrs Methuselah.'

'And look it,' said Bill, his eyes twinkling.

As she gave him a playful swat with the paperback she been reading, Janet asked, 'Did you hear Diane scream?'

'No, I didn't. What time was that?'

'Just after two. Diane woke up, put her torch on to see what the time was, and was horrified to see a large cockroach on the bulkhead by her pillow. I'm surprised you didn't hear her yell for help. You must be a very sound sleeper.'

'Usually—yes,' Charlotte agreed. There had been someone shouting in one of her dreams, she remembered.

'The Professor was the first on the scene. He seems to read half the night and was already awake. Then Manik arrived, followed by Dean and me and, eventually, by my sloth of a husband. It was like Piccadilly Underground station in the rush hour down there last night, wasn't it, Dean?' as he joined them.

He grinned and nodded.

'It took me ages to calm Diane down,' Janet went on. 'I thought it best not to tell her that although the cockroach she saw was caught and despatched, there are probably lots more in hiding. It's inevitable in this climate. It isn't because the crew aren't cleaning the boat properly. The galley is spotless—I've looked.'

'Poor Diane. Let's hope the next thing she sees isn't a shark,' said Bill. 'Although the sharks in these waters are supposed to be friendly, so I've read.'

'I'd as soon not put that to the test,' Dean said drily. 'Is it true that Maldivian sharks don't eat people, Skipper?'

Manik, on his way to the stern, paused. 'The sharks are not hungry...they have many fish to eat. The dangers for tourists are strong currents and, when the wind is strong, big waves hitting the reef. Also, when snorkelling, it is better only to look, not to touch. Some coral stings. You will come to no harm if you do what is advised.'

As he said this he glanced at Charlotte, and she felt sure he was referring to his warning to her last night.

'What's the programme today?' Bill asked him. 'Are we staying here or moving on?'

They had been given an itinerary with their travel documents, but it had been emphasised that their route around the atoll would depend on the weather and could be changed at the discretion of the skipper.

'Today we go to very small island . . . very good snorkelling,' said Manik.

The next few days were uneventful. Charlotte made friends with Janet whom, in spite of the age gap between them, she found a pleasant companion.

To their mutual surprise and amusement, Diane and the Professor seemed to have struck up an unlikely friendship.

'What in the world do they find to talk about?' Janet pondered aloud, watching them sauntering along a beach together. 'Still, I suppose she's realised that Dean is out of reach, and that only leaves the Professor.'

'Why is Dean out of reach?' asked Charlotte.

'It would take more than spectacular vital statistics to attract him. A man of his sophistication demands intelligence and character as well as a beautiful body,' Janet said sagely.

'Isn't the Professor sophisticated?'

'Being clever isn't the same thing. Clever men are often quite childish outside their particular field. Not that I think the Professor's interest in her, or hers in him, is more than a temporary expedient. He's enjoying the undulations of all that voluptuous flesh, and for Diane any man's better than none.'

'Surely our skipper is a more attractive man than the Professor?' said Charlotte.

'Manik? Yes, but he's very reserved. He's polite and he answers our questions, but he isn't being really friendly. He keeps a distance between us...more than he does with his crew. I don't think Diane would get anywhere with him, and she knows it.'

Charlotte wondered if Janet, who seemed both observant and shrewd, had any inkling of how things stood between Dean and Manik and herself.

Since the visit to the Italian resort, she had done her best to avoid finding herself in a tête-à-tête situation with either man. She felt now that at Boduhithi her relationship with Dean had gone too far too fast. There were girls who let men make love to them on the strength of a single dinner date, but she had never been one of them, and, although she had enjoyed it while it was happening, now she half regretted the enthusiasm with which she had kissed him.

At the same time—and she knew this to be irrational—she was slightly piqued that he had made no further move. She felt sure it was not beyond the bounds of his ingenuity to get her alone if he wanted to, but it seemed that he didn't.

Perhaps he regretted the impulse which had prompted him to kiss her. Perhaps he was the kind of man who was put off by women who responded too readily. If he thought her a sitting duck, he might have lost interest, preferring women who, at least in the early stages, played hard to get.

CHAPTER EIGHT

THE accident happened the day they dropped anchor
not far from a reef which might one day might emerge
from the ocean and become an island.

At present it was merely a group of corals in a patch
of shallow water which, from the deck of the schooner
as they approached it, looked like a bowl of pale emerald
jelly which had been stirred before it was properly set.

It was necessary to anchor in deep water some distance from where they were going to snorkel and to go
to the reef in the dinghy. Awaiting her turn to climb down
the ladder, Charlotte chanced to glance round and saw
that they must be somewhere in the centre of the atoll.
There were only two islands in sight and, the day being
humid and hazy, they were almost lost to view on the
horizon.

It crossed her mind that they were a long way from
land. Not a good place to be on a *dhoni* in the treach-
erous weather in Funors, but safe enough now in the
settled climate of Dinasha.

Diane, the Professor, Olly and Janet had decided to
stay on board, but everyone else was going to the reef,
including Sylvia, who wanted to take some pictures of
Stanley snorkelling. Although, as Vic murmured to
Charlotte, people face-down in the sea didn't make exciting photographs.

While Maumoon, the boatman, and Sylvia remained
in the dinghy, the others went over the side to gaze
through their masks at the fascinating world beneath the
surface.

126

For Charlotte the reefs were like a familiar landscape to a countryman. The shapes of the corals, the many species of fish were not strange to her as they were to the others. She thought her response must be similar to that of an English gardener after a long exile in a country where roses did not grow and only crab-grass would flourish, not the soft green plush of English lawns. Even in the Caribbean, where she had snorkelled many times, around most of the larger islands the corals were not as luxuriant, the fish not as numerous as here.

Manik had told them to keep together and to return to the dinghy after half an hour. The time sped, and soon Vic was tapping his waterproof watch to signal that their time was up.

It was as they were converging on the dinghy and Sylvia was preparing to snap them that she suddenly lost her balance and fell backwards. As she fell, Maumoon, the boatman, jumped up with a cry of alarm, their combined movements making the dinghy rock sideways like a cradle.

'Stupid woman! If she's damaged my new camera, I'll have something to say!' exclaimed Stanley.

Charlotte thought it more likely that Sylvia had damaged herself. Had it been imagination, or had she heard a nasty crack as his wife had disappeared from view?

The first man to hoist himself inboard was Dean, whose powerful muscles made it an easy exercise. Bill followed, then Vic, then Charlotte, with Maumoon having to help Stanley who, spending his life in a local government office, had no strength in his arms.

Seeing Sylvia lying with closed eyes where she had fallen, Charlotte thought it would be Dean who would take charge of the situation. But it was Bill who informed them briskly that he was a doctor and who bent over the unconscious woman, while the others took off their masks and Maumoon lost no time in starting the motor to return to the schooner.

In his first moments in the dinghy, Stanley seemed more worried about the dropped camera than about Sylvia's condition. Until he saw Bill's hand come away from the back of her head covered with bright blood, and uttered a shaken, 'Good God!'

'Don't flap. Head injuries always bleed profusely,' said Bill. 'She may come round in a minute.'

But Sylvia was still unconscious when, with some difficulty, they lifted her on board *Sea Bird* and, following Bill's instructions, laid her gently on the deck with a bathing towel under her still-bleeding head.

Bill had shouted to Janet as they came alongside, and it was soon apparent that she was used to dealing with this kind of contingency.

'Is it serious, sir?' The question came from Manik as he watched Bill and his wife stanching the flow of blood and re-checking Sylvia's vital signs.

'Any concussion... any head injury may be serious. How far are we from a hospital with X-ray and surgery facilities?'

'The hospital is at Malé... five hours from here.'

'Then you'd better radio for help... get her taken off by helicopter,' said Bill.

'Yes, sir.'

As Manik turned to carry out Bill's instruction, Stanley grabbed his arm. 'Wait a minute! What's a helicopter going to cost? My insurance may not cover——'

'Whatever it costs, in my opinion it's necessary,' Bill cut in. He signalled to Manik to go ahead. 'Your wife needs an X-ray and stitches, Stanley. It's possible she may need an operation. Stuck out here in the middle of an atoll, we can't afford to take chances... even if she'd come round almost immediately.'

Dean said, 'Don't worry about the expense, Neasden. The travel company will pick up the tab. Jardine Latimer have a reputation for looking after their customers in circumstances such as these. You won't find yourself landed with a massive bill.'

At that moment Sylvia moaned and her eyelids flickered.

'Look, she's coming round,' said Stanley. 'Surely it isn't necessary to send for a helicopter? If we start now, we can be at Malé by——'

'You're not thinking clearly,' Dean said incisively. 'There are other people on board. They don't want to go to Malé. They want to continue their holiday.'

'But we're going to spend a day there anyway. What difference does it make if we go there today or next week?'

'It's likely that your wife will be kept in hospital for observation. Am I right, Bill?' said Dean. When the other man nodded, he went on, 'If Sylvia's recovered by the time we get to Malé, you can both come back on board and continue the cruise. But although we're all sympathetic, I'm afraid it's unreasonable to expect the whole itinerary to be changed because of what's happened.'

A few minutes later Manik reported that the helicopter was on its way.

Looking relieved, Bill said, 'Help Stanley pack, will you, Janet? If I were you, I should take all your gear with you, Stanley. Then, in the event that Sylvia needs extended treatment or doesn't feel up to continuing the trip, you'll have it with you.'

'But——' Stanley began to protest.

'Come along, Stanley. The helicopter may be here quite soon, and we don't want to keep it waiting,' said Janet kindly but firmly.

When she had taken him below, Dean said to Bill, 'I take it you'll be going with them, Bill? Handing her over to one of your Maldivian colleagues?'

The doctor nodded. 'In case the helicopter can't bring me back immediately, I'd better have some overnight things with me. Pop down and remind Janet that I'll need my wash pack and a clean shirt, will you, Charlotte?'

'I'll tell her. I'm going below to throw a few things together for myself,' said Dean. 'I think I'd better come with you, Bill. I have some contacts in London who may be useful if it's necessary to pull any strings.'

When he had gone, Charlotte signed to Manik that she wanted to speak to him out of earshot of the others. After they had withdrawn to the stern, she said, 'Ought I go with them, do you think? Is it advisable to have someone who speaks Dhivehi with them?'

'No, no...they speak English at the hospital. You will not be needed there,' he said. 'I don't like the look of the woman. A violent blow on the head is a very dangerous injury. I think her skull is fractured and there is damage to the brain. She may need an operation to save her.'

Charlotte thought the same. Sylvia still had not recovered full consciousness. She had opened her eyes, but with no sign of knowing where she was or what had happened. After muttering that her head hurt, she had slipped back into an inert state.

Although the waiting time dragged, it was actually not long before the helicopter could be seen and heard approaching. Equipped with floats, it landed not far from schooner's anchorage. Charlotte didn't care to contemplate what transferring Sylvia to it would have been like had the sea been choppy. But it was almost flat calm, and very soon the patient and her husband, and the two other men, were starting their flight to the capital.

Those left behind on *Sea Bird* waved as the helicopter took off and headed south. Manik had already given orders for the crew to make sail. The itinerary had been changed. Instead of spending the night lying off a small uninhabited island, they were going to a resort he called Meeru, short for Meerufenfushi, meaning Sweet Water.

That evening, while they were ashore, Janet was called to the telephone.

When she rejoined the others who were sitting round a table on the sand outside the island's main bar, she said, 'That was Bill. Sylvia's condition has improved. She's been X-rayed and had the wound stitched and now she's on a drip, under observation for forty-eight hours. Bill and Dean are staying overnight, mainly as moral support for Stanley. They'll be back in the morning.'

'Poor old Sylvia! I bet, as soon as she's better, she'll get it in the neck from Stanley,' said Olly. 'What a drag that man is! If he were my husband, I'd slip some arsenic in his tea!'

'Did Bill say where they were spending the night, Janet?' asked Charlotte.

'Some guesthouse . . . clean but rather basic, I gather. There aren't any hotels as such in Malé, he says.'

'Sylvia was lucky to have a doctor on the spot,' said Vic.

'I'm sure if Bill hadn't been here, you or Dean or Manik would have coped very well. Or, for that matter, Olly or Charlotte,' said Janet. Perhaps with the thought in her mind that the two people not present might not have coped so well, she said, 'Where are the others?'

'They're in the other bar,' said Olly. 'The Prof's got a clean shirt on—how about that? He's really smitten with Diane, but I'd like to know what her game is. She can't fancy him, that's for sure. Maybe she likes the idea of an easy life with a few students on the side.'

'You'll get had up for libel one of these days, Ol,' said Vic. 'Or do I mean slander? Drink up, ladies. It's my round.'

Later, when they were back on board, Janet said to Charlotte, 'It seems strange without Bill.'

Charlotte had been thinking that it would seem strange sleeping on deck without Dean on the other side of the rope box.

She said, 'You're very lucky to be so happily married. It must be a great relationship when two people get on as well as you and Bill obviously do.'

'It's not just luck, my dear,' Janet said drily. 'A lot more people could be happily married if they worked harder at it...and used more common sense in their choice of partners in the first place.'

'How did you and Bill meet?' asked Charlotte.

'I was a first-year nurse and he was a medical student. Some of the other students were much better looking and had lots of the nurses mad about them. But Bill had a kind heart—that's the thing to look for in a husband. Do you know the old-fashioned saying: Kisses don't last, cookery do? Applied to men, I'd substitute kindness for cookery.'

Charlotte would have liked to ask her if she thought Dean a kind man. It had seemed an act of great kindness for him to accompany the others to Malé in case there was anything he could do to help.

Later, preparing for bed, she wondered about the contacts he had mentioned.

The schooner was moored closer to the beach than at any of the other islands they had visited, and the taped music playing in the bar and the sound of voices and laughter were still going on when those aboard *Sea Bird* bade each other goodnight.

A few minutes after Charlotte had stretched herself out on her mattress, Manik appeared. Normally he and the crew never came forward at night. She sat up, wondering why he had come now, when Dean was absent.

Speaking Dhivehi, his voice low, he said, 'Don't be afraid, I am not going to touch you.'

He dropped down on his haunches. Tonight, for the first time, he was wearing the traditional *lungi* of checked cotton, indigo on brown, or so the colours appeared in the moonlight.

'You are angry with me for what I did at Boduhithi?' It might have been a statement or a question.

'It was you who was angry with me, Manik,' Charlotte reminded him.

'How else should a man feel when the woman he wants is embraced by another man . . . with her consent? But I should have shown my anger to him, not to you.'

Charlotte was taken aback. Was Manik telling her he loved her?

Before she could answer, he surprised her again by saying, 'Maumoon blames himself for the accident this afternoon. I have told him it was not his fault. He thinks the woman will die. He says no one could hit their head with such force and live. And she is not a strong, healthy woman.'

Confused by this complete change of subject, she said, 'I don't see how Maumoon, or you, could possibly be held responsible for the accident.'

'A master is responsible for everything that happens while he is at sea. If Neasden's woman must have an expensive operation, or if he demands compensation, the owners of *Sea Bird* will not be pleased.'

'Surely they must be insured against these eventualities?' she queried.

'Without doubt, but even so they will not like it. Maumoon is worried. He has five children to feed. He fears the owners may order me to replace him.'

'If they do, you won't agree to it, will you?'

He shook his head. 'No; but the owners are business-men...hard men, concerned only with profit. They could dismiss me as well. There are many who would be glad to take my place as skipper.'

'I doubt if there are many who have your long ex-perience at sea *and* speak such good English,' said Charlotte. 'The tour operator's brochure stresses that point...that the skipper of *Sea Bird* speaks English. They're the people the owners have to worry about.'

'That's true. But the girl who met you at the airport tells me me that the company she works for—the company which charters *Sea Bird* from the owners—has changed hands. It has been bought by a more important company. I have forgotten the name, but——'

'Jardine Latimer,' said Charlotte. 'A name well known in Europe...as well known as Thomas Cook or P & O. As a matter of fact, they're now my employers. I told you I worked for a travel company...well, it was the one which has just been taken over by Jardine Latimer.'

'So you know more about them than the Australian, Liz?' queried Manik.

'Not really...only what everyone knows. They've been in the travel business for almost a hundred years. When Grandfather was a young man, he used them. They're a family firm handed down from father to son, and each generation has improved the business. The present Jardine Latimer is said to be one of the richest men in Britain, but he keeps out of the public eye.'

'To a man such as that, the price of a boat like this would be nothing...as unimportant as a few *larees* to me,' said Manik, referring to the smallest coins of the country's currency, each one representing a hundredth part of a *rufiya*. 'If I could talk to such a man, he might lend me the money to buy a schooner of my own. But he is as distant from me as the stars——' looking up at the night sky.

'You could write to him,' said Charlotte.

'Rich men are sent many letters from people wanting money. He will have a secretary—two or three secretaries—who will deal with those letters. Mine would never be seen by his eyes.'

'It might be, if the secretary thought your proposal had merit. What have you got to lose? Only the cost of an envelope and a stamp? If you like, I'll help you write it,' said Charlotte.

Manik rose to his feet. 'I will think about it.' He looked down at her for a moment. 'The others call you Charlotte, and this is also the name you have written in the drinks book. You are not called Pet now?'

'Charlotte is my baptismal name,' she explained. 'When I first went away to school in England, it took some time to get used to being called Charlotte. No one has called me Pet since Grandfather died.'

'He was a good old man. Without him, I should be nothing, even though my mother's people were *befalu*,' he said.

The *befalu* were an upper, privileged class of Maldivians, at the opposite end of the social scale from the Givaru, descendants of the islands' early settlers from Southern India, who had always been treated as inferiors.

'Whichever way your life had gone, you would always have been a man to respect,' said Charlotte. 'Don't you remember Grandfather telling us, when we were children, that the only kind of respect worth having is self-respect?'

'Yes, I remember. But I did not have respect for myself after I had kissed you at Boduhithi. A man should never use his strength to make a woman submit to him. I am sorry for that.'

'I accept your apology. It's forgotten,' she said gravely.

'Not by me,' said Manik. 'I shall never forget the first time I felt your lips under mine. Goodnight, Pet . . . Charlotte.'

* * *

Very early in the morning, before it was fully light, Charlotte slipped over the side and swam ashore with her sarong and an orange in a plastic bag. As she had on the first morning of the cruise, she wanted to explore the perimeter of the island, which was considerably larger than the one she had walked round that other day.

Although she had lain awake for a long time after Manik had left her, when at last she had dropped off she had slept well, without dreaming. As she walked along the beach, past a line of single-storey bedrooms with small verandas, and past the island's wind-surfing centre with its racks of boards and brightly coloured plastic sails, she wondered what sort of night Dean and Bill had had in their guesthouse in Malé, and whether they would be back later today.

Although she couldn't raise much sympathy for Stanley, she did feel sorry for Sylvia who at best would be feeling very poorly and, at worst, might be spending the morning in an operating theatre.

Once, while she was working in Spain, Charlotte had been the only person available to spend a night in hospital with an elderly tourist who had broken her leg. In that particular hospital, as in many others in Spain, only medical attention had been provided. All other care had been the responsibility of the patients' families. Until Mrs Shadwell's son and daughter-in-law had arrived to take over, she had been dependent on Charlotte for all her other needs.

A few weeks later, a magnificent canteen of Victorian silver cutlery had been sent to Charlotte care of the managing director of her firm, with a letter to him from Mrs Shadwell, praising Charlotte's kindness. Another note of thanks, addressed to Charlotte herself, had explained that the cutlery had been a wedding present to Mrs Shadwell's grandmother from the lady for whom she had worked as a personal maid. Mrs Shadwell's daughter-in-law didn't like old things, but Amy Shadwell knew from their conversations that Charlotte did, and also that she had a young man. The canteen was for her bottom drawer, with her benefactor's most grateful thanks.

And in Charlotte's bottom drawer, or rather in the strongroom at her bank, it had remained, the young man having proved a disappointment.

Remembering the ornate set of silver—six place settings bedded in dark green velvet in a heavy mahogany case—and wondering when if ever she would use them, brought Charlotte's thoughts back to Manik's statements last night.

'How else should a man feel when the woman he wants is embraced by another man? I shall never forget the first time I felt your lips under mine.'

Was she to take it that he loved her and wanted to marry her? If so, why had he walked away without expressing his feelings even more plainly, without kissing her again?

But if he had, what would she have said? How would she have responded? She didn't know. And the reason she didn't know was that there was another man who had made her pulses race and whose presence she missed.

Towards the northern end of Meerufenfushi the beach widened into a broad expanse of sand curving round to the eastern side of the island. Here she came across a tourist setting up his easel to paint the line of fallen palms, their roots like huge untidy rooks' nests, over whose trunks she had had to clamber. She guessed they had been brought down by strong winds and high tides in June.

She was wearing her plastic reef-walking shoes, which was just as well, because on the far side of the island she had to wade over rocks and past thickets of man-

groves overhanging the water. Here the air was full of
golden dragonflies.

This had once been her world, and its hold on her
heart was still very strong. So strong that for seven years
her ambition had been to come back, to be promoted
to a resort island manager. Which was what she had
done. When the voyage came to an end, she would be
replacing a manager who wanted to return to Europe.
It was the first time the company she worked for had
appointed a woman to such a plum position.

It was what she had wanted all along, the reason for
years of putting her job first, often to the detriment of
her private life.

Yet now, when the prize had been won, suddenly she
had doubts. *Was* this where she belonged? Or was her
heart now in Europe, or if not in Europe, with a man
who lived there; a man who, if she stayed here, she would
never see again?

Presently Charlotte found herself passing some more
bedrooms, all with their curtains drawn. What a waste,
she thought, to come all this way and miss the best part
of the day lying in bed, hot and sticky, when out here
the air was fresh and the light was still gentle.

Not far from Meerufenfushi, across a channel of deep
water, was another island. Manik had told her it was
inhabited by Maldivians. Although it was an easy swim,
tourists from Meeru were discouraged from going there.
She wondered if her Dhivehi, still a bit rusty from long
disuse, would ensure a welcome for her if she swam over.
She decided she had better not.

Her thoughts jumped to Malé... Malé where, at this
moment, Dean might be shaving or having his morning
shower. A mental picture of him standing naked in the
shower stall, soapsuds streaming down his long lithe body
as he washed his dark hair, sent a strange little shudder
through her.

But was the attraction he had for her purely physical? Or could there be more, much more, between them?

The voyage was already half over. There was so little time left.

At breakfast, Vic said, 'I reckon they'll come back on the *dhoni* which is taking some people from here on a day trip to Malé. So we shan't see them till this evening...that's if it's all gone smoothly.'

At mid-morning a different helicopter appeared in the sky, reminding Charlotte of the dragonflies she had seen on her walk round Meerufenfushi.

When she realised it was not on its way to one of the other islands but was coming to Meeru, her heart leapt...and then plummeted at the thought that it might not be Dean coming back, but an unknown VIP or someone to do with the management of the island.

The helicopter landed on the football pitch. She saw it touch down. Its passengers were Dean and Bill.

'What news?' she asked, as they came towards her.

'Not bad,' said Bill. 'Sylvia's not out of the woods yet, but she's making a better recovery than I expected yesterday, and I'm satisfied that she's in competent hands.'

Janet came hurrying up. While she and Bill greeted each other, Dean said, 'What's this island like? Looks good from the air.'

'The island itself is delightful. The blocks of rooms have been built as cheaply as possible and, from glimpses I've had, are pretty basic inside,' Charlotte told him. 'But I don't imagine your accommodation last night was anything to write home about.'

'It could have been worse. When there was nothing more we could do for the Neasdens, Bill and I had an interesting potter round the town—the shops stay open late—and an excellent curry in a restaurant down by the wharves. I bought you a present. If it's not the right size, or if you don't like it, there'll be a chance to change it when we all go to Malé.'

Dean fished in the flight bag he had taken with him and produced a floppy parcel.

'How very kind of you,' said Charlotte. 'May I open it now?'

'Why not?'

The wrapping was secured with bits of sticky tape. It didn't take long to discover that his gift was a shirt made of pieces of *batik* cotton patchworked together.

'I bought two... one for my mother. It's the sort of thing she likes to wear when she's painting,' said Dean.

'It's lovely!' said Charlotte excitedly, slipping it on. 'I admired some of these in the shop at Boduhithi. I'm sure your mother will be delighted...and so am I. Thank you, Dean.'

To her surprise, he bent his head, turning his face sideways in a clear invitation. Although now Bill and Janet were watching, she had no choice but to brush a light kiss on his tanned cheek.

'That's very snazzy,' said Janet, admiring the shirt. 'If you can remember where you found it, Dean, I might get a couple for our girls. Why didn't you buy some for them, Bill?'

'I wasn't sure it was the kind of thing they like. Usually when I buy anything for the females in my life, they tell me it's awful and take it back and change it,' he told the others, smiling. 'Also Dean is an expert haggler, which I'm not,' he added, to his wife. 'The man in the shop where he bought those wanted twenty dollars. Dean beat him down to——' A nudge from Janet made him pause. 'Oh, sorry, nearly put my foot in it. Still, it's the thought that counts, not the price, isn't it, Charlotte?'

'Absolutely,' she agreed. 'And, being a great haggler myself, I should have thought less of Dean if he had paid the asking price. Which, as it happens, was half what they wanted for these on Boduhithi. By the time they reach London, as I expect they will, they'll be even more expensive.'

She slipped the shirt off and folded it.

'So how was Stanley bearing up when you left him?' asked Janet.

'Not pleased at being deserted, but, as Dean said they would, the tour operators are behaving very well. Sylvia will have to spend another night or two in hospital to make sure there's nothing bad happening inside her skull. But the indications are good, and when they discharge her she and Stanley will be transferred to an island called Bandos to spend the rest of their holiday there. We shan't see them again until the flight back to London.'

It was Manik who, when this information was relayed to him, said, 'In that case, Miss Charlotte can now have her cabin to herself. You will move your luggage to the empty cabin, if you please, sir.'

In spite of the 'sir' he tacked on, it was unmistakably an order, and Charlotte wondered if Dean might bristle at being addressed in that tone by someone who, perhaps unconsciously, he regarded as his inferior.

But his easy, 'Will do, Skipper,' held no hint of sarcasm. It made her feel that perhaps, like her grandfather, he was one of those rare people who judged all human beings on their merits as individuals, regardless of any other factors.

'If you don't want to use the cabin for a bit, I'll go down and do it now,' he added to Charlotte.

It seemed strange, that evening, when she went below to put on clean clothes for dinner, to find only her own things in the cabin. She had grown accustomed to the sight of Dean's shirts in the hanging locker, his books and other belongings on the upper bunk. She felt an odd sense of loss.

The following afternoon, after they had anchored off
another island and, later, were going ashore to be shown
a dried fish warehouse and walk round a Maldivian
village, Charlotte went below to dress in a way which
would not offend the islanders' ideas of modesty.

She had taken off her shorts and sun-top and was
brushing her hair, naked but for a pair of blue cotton
micro-panties, her shore-going outfit still in the locker,
when the door suddenly opened. Startled, she stood with
her brushing arm momentarily frozen.

It was Dean who had opened the door. He looked
equally taken aback at the sight of her.

'Oh...sorry...force of habit,' he said, after a second
or two. 'Forgot I'd moved.'

But his apology wasn't followed by a rapid retreat.
Instead his grey eyes swept slowly over her body in a
look that made her catch her breath.

His next action was to close the door, but not with
him on the other side of it. When the catch clicked into
place, he was inside the cabin with her.

CHAPTER NINE

IT WAS the first time they had been shut in the cabin together. The confined space accentuated Dean's size. As he leaned back against it, his shoulders were as broad as the door. The deckhead was only an inch or two above his thick dark hair which, still damp from a recent swim and casually raked back with his fingers—a gesture Charlotte knew well by now—made him look younger.

The impression was emphasised by the faded blue denim shorts which sat low on his hips, exposing the tight curl of his navel and a midriff still as flat and hard as if he were twenty.

The latent power implicit in every line of his lean, deeply suntanned body made her feel frail by comparison. But strangely, in spite of her nakedness and the absence of anything at hand to snatch up and cover herself, she felt neither nervous nor embarrassed.

He said quietly, 'Swinburne wrote a poem about you. "And all her face was honey to my mouth, And all her body pasture to mine eyes".'

As he said the lines, his eyes caressed her and, to her amazement, she found her body responding as if he were actually stroking her shoulders, her breasts, her waist, her hips, her thighs.

It was the strangest sensation she had experienced. No one had ever made love to her with his voice and his eyes before, nor would she have thought it possible to feel such a strong surge of pleasure without any physical contact.

But apparently, with Dean, it was, and, hardly knowing what she was doing, acting on some deep instinct beyond her conscious control, slowly she lowered her arm, put the brush on her bunk and stood waiting, her breathing uneven, for whatever he chose to do next.

For a long tense moment their eyes met. In his she recognised the glitter of desire and knew that her eyes must be sending him the same signal.

Then Dean lunged away from the door and an instant later she was locked in his arms, their bare torsos pressed together in a delicious union of his hardness and her softness, their mouths hungrily kissing.

'I'm going down to put on a skirt. I shan't be long.'

It was Janet's voice, from the deck overhead, which made Charlotte open her eyes and return to a world in which other people existed; not just Dean and herself, lost in a kind of delirium.

It was only as they drew apart that she realised that, even with the fan on, they were both glistening with moisture. But until Janet's voice had disturbed them, neither had been aware of the heat or their cramped surroundings. The only reality had been their desire for each other.

'It sounds as if the trip ashore is starting sooner than we thought. I'd better get out of here. We'll talk later,' Dean said huskily.

He brushed a light kiss on her cheek and a moment later was gone.

Whether anyone saw him leaving her cabin, Charlotte neither knew nor cared. She longed to collapse on her bunk and recover from the storm of emotion. Or, better still, to dive into the refreshing coolness of the sea.

Instead she wrapped herself in a towel and slipped into the washroom to have a rapid rinse down.

The others were either in the dinghy or waiting their turn on the ladder when she went on deck. In a quick glance at Dean she saw that he looked as calm as if he had spent the past half-hour discussing rationalism with the Professor.

Perhaps she looked equally composed. But she didn't feel it. In Dean's arms she had discovered a new self, a creature without inhibitions. She had never felt like that before, or only in her private fantasies, not in real life. But then none of the men she had known had been as demanding as Dean, or as tender. The way he made love had been a revelation.

Manik was standing below her as she climbed over the side, her navy cotton culottes making it easier for her than the skirts worn by the other women. He looked annoyed about something, and for a moment she wondered if he knew Dean had been in her cabin and had advanced the going-ashore time to curtail whatever he suspected of happening.

'What are those, Skipper?' asked Vic, pointing to several square frames, formed from bamboo poles lashed together, which were floating on the surface of the lagoon, one of them with a reef heron perching on it.

Manik's expression cleared slightly. 'They are storage nets for the fishermen's bait-fish,' he explained.

Their arrival at the island's jetty was watched by a group of men sitting in the shade of a large banyan tree whose aerial roots, growing down from the branches, made it look like a group of trees. A primitive swing-seat had been made from a lopped branch and *jolis* had also been slung from the tree on ropes.

It was mid-afternoon and very hot walking along a dusty road to the warehouse stacked high with pungent dried tuna ready for export.

'Phew, what a stink! Good thing Stanley's not here. He wouldn't like the pong from that lot,' said Olly.

When they arrived at the village with its white coral-sand roads, coral-stone walls and coral-built houses, Charlotte was reminded of Thabu, although there the majority of houses had been timber-framed and thatched instead of, as here, roofed with corrugated iron.

Presently they came to a shop selling shells and T-shirts. While his party looked at the souvenirs, Manik talked to one of the islanders. When a small boy came running up, he bent to rumple the child's curls and to give him a sweet from his pocket.

In their progress about the village, it was noticeable that he liked children and they liked him, the boys obviously feeling some hero-worship for the captain of a vessel as fine as *Sea Bird* and the girls in their teens sneaking admiring glances at him.

Charlotte had avoided looking at Dean while they were going round the island. She felt sure that if she did her face would reveal her feelings.

We'll talk later, he had said. But when? This evening those who wanted to try their hand at night-fishing would have the chance to catch a fish for their supper. But not everyone would go. So even if she and Dean opted out, they wouldn't be left alone.

Privacy was in short supply on board *Sea Bird*. Even the married couples, if they didn't want their conversation overheard through the open deck lights or thin partitions, had to talk in undertones.

In the event they both went on the night-fishing trip, leaving Olly and Diane and the Professor aboard. But nobody had a catch.

It was when they returned to the schooner and the others were going below to tidy themselves for the evening meal that Dean touched Charlotte's arm and murmured, 'Let's go for'ard for five minutes.'

In the bows, he said in a low voice, 'This is an impossible situation. I want to have you to myself.

Tomorrow we're going to Malé. Why don't we jump ship?'

'To go where?' she asked.

'The island called Kudahithi is supposed to be a good place for people who want to be alone.'

'*Millionaires* who want to be alone,' Charlotte corrected. 'I couldn't afford Kudahithi.'

'OK, we'll find somewhere less expensive.' Dean bent his head till his lips were close to her ear. 'I don't care what it's like as long as you're there with me and we have some privacy.'

The passion in his voice sent a shiver of longing down her spine. She wanted, as much as he did, to be somewhere where they could make love. But she wanted more. She wanted to know that he loved her; that he wanted her heart and soul, not merely her body.

'I don't know,' she said uncertainly. 'We're already two people short. If you and I drop out as well...'

'This isn't a private yacht party. We aren't someone's guests. There's no obligation to stay.'

'I know, but... but Manik won't like it.'

'Manik? What the devil has he got to do with it?'

'I—I shouldn't like him to think that all Europeans are... immoral, which he would if I went off with you.'

'I don't give a damn what Manik thinks,' said Dean, with a touch of impatience. 'And I doubt if he gives a toss for my opinion. Are you trying to tell me it would bother *you* to spend the rest of your holiday alone with me?'

To avoid answering that, she said, 'You don't understand. Well, how could you, when I haven't told you? You see, I've been here before... in fact, I grew up here. Manik and I were friends when we were children. That's why what he thinks does matter to me.'

'I see. That explains a lot. But it doesn't alter the fact that your actions should be guided only by what you think right, not by anyone else's code of behaviour. If you don't want to spend time with me, that's up to you. But don't make Manik your excuse for backing off.'

'I'm not backing off,' said Charlotte. 'I—I just don't want to rush into something I might regret.'

Dean rested his wrist on her shoulder and began stroking her neck with the tips of his fingers.

'You're not a dizzy teenager, Charlotte. You're a grown-up, sensible woman. Why not go on trusting your instincts? You did this afternoon. You came into my arms as if you belonged there.'

The reminder of her eager response, and the feel of his fingers and thumb exploring soft places behind her ear and the line of her jaw, made her long to be back in his arms with her lips parting under his.

'Don't rush me, Dean. I need time to think,' she said huskily. 'If you——' She broke off.

He took away his hand. 'If I...what?'

'Do you remember Liz, the Australian girl who met us at Malé?' she asked.

'I do, but I don't see how she comes into this.'

'I earn my living the same way as she does. What I was going to say was that if you'd seen as many people as I have make fools of themselves on holiday, you'd know that it's fatally easy to...to get carried away.'

'I know that,' he said. 'I'm thirty-five, I've been carried away a few times. I expect you have too. That's the reason I think we should spend the rest of our time here together. We've a lot to find out about each other before this holiday ends and we go back to Europe and our everyday lives.'

'It takes much longer than two weeks to find out what another person is really like,' she said. 'I'm not certain that our going off together would prove anything. I'm sure it would be...very enjoyable. But that could make saying goodbye more painful...especially for me. Men walk away from these things a lot more easily than women do.'

He said softly, 'There's also the possibility that we might not say goodbye.'

Then the ship's bell summoned them to dinner.

During the meal, Janet said, 'It's quite blowy tonight. I'm going to fetch a wrap.'

Until then Charlotte had been too preoccupied to notice that the edges of the awning were flapping and the wind was plucking the shrouds like an inexpert hand on the strings of an untuned mandolin.

In the saloon, the crew had been listening to a local radio station. While the passengers were having coffee, Manik appeared.

'It will be windy tonight...too windy to sleep on deck. You will sleep in your cabins, please,' glancing at Charlotte and Dean. 'Tomorrow we go to Malé, where you can shop and visit the mosque and museum. There is also a duty-free shop, but other passengers tell me they do not find bargains there.' He shrugged. 'You must judge for yourselves. But the ladies do not have to worry that they will be robbed or molested. Malé is a safe place.'

'It doesn't look a safe place to me,' Diane said apprehensively when, the following morning, the dinghy was cruising along Malé's waterfront with Maumoon looking for a landing-place.

Between the sea-wall and the wharves, the harbour was criss-crossed by mooring lines which Ahmed, the assistant boatman, lifted before the dinghy passed under them. Even so the passengers had to crouch down.

Charlotte could see that for someone like Diane, who had no previous experience of Eastern ports, the place might look rather sinister. Among the many *dhonis* were the larger vessels called *vedis* which had come from the outer atolls and had palm-thatched roofs in various stages of dilapidation. There were few women to be seen. Many of the men were unshaven, barefoot and rather villainous-looking.

To Charlotte, who had come here many times with her grandfather to pick up mail and provisions, the docks at Malé and the narrow alleys behind them were full of excitement and interest.

But the great golden onion-like dome of a large mosque, and the smaller gold dome of its tall minaret from which, five times a day, the faithful would be called to their prayers, had not existed in those days.

Eventually Maumoon found a space by the fish market and Manik told everyone to come back to the harbour at one o'clock for lunch on board, after which those who wished could return for a second look round.

'Oh, no! Don't say we've got to go through all that three more times!' wailed Diane.

The sea was choppy this morning and, with the dinghy heaving and lurching, she had been terrified of falling between it and the schooner's hull. Even with both Dean and Manik there to catch her if she slipped, she had been close to hysteria by the time they got her safely inboard. But for the lure of the shops, she would have stayed on the schooner.

'Don't worry, my dear. I'm sure there's somewhere to have lunch ashore, and the wind may have dropped by this evening,' said the Professor. 'I suggest we go and find a coffee shop where you can recover yourself.'

'That would be lovely, Paddy,' Diane said gratefully. She peered in a mirror inside the flap of her shoulder-bag, exclaiming with horror at the sight of her tear-smudged eye make-up.

'Aren't you coming to the hospital to see how Sylvia's getting on?' asked Janet.

'I don't think we will. She won't want a whole crowd of visitors, will she? You can give her our regards,' Diane said airily.

They found Sylvia up and dressed, sitting on a shady veranda. She was alone. Stanley was sightseeing. That afternoon they were going to the resort where she would complete her convalescence.

'They've certainly done a nice job of sewing you up,' said Bill, inspecting the area of scalp which, shorn of hair, was covered with a film of artificial skin through which could be seen a neat line of stitches.

'Typical of Stanley to leave her by herself,' said Janet, on their way out of the hospital. 'Hello, look who's here. Where did you get those beautiful flowers, Manik?'

'I have a friend in Malé whose garden is full of flowers. I asked his wife if she would give me some for Mrs Neasden,' he explained. 'How is she today?'

Janet told him, and a few moments later he went to find Sylvia and the others started to walk back to the centre of town.

'That was a kind thought,' said Janet. 'I'm a little surprised that Dean didn't come with us. I wouldn't expect Diane to put herself out for anyone, but I should have thought Dean would make the effort.'

'That's not quite fair, dear,' said Bill. 'He came here the day it happened, remember. It was his idea to fax the news of the accident to London, so to some extent the Neasdens have him to thank for the excellent re-arrangements. And I was very glad of his company that night, I must say.'

Dean had gone off on his own and they did not see him until they returned to the rendezvous point, where Manik announced that because the wind was stronger now, and the sea rougher, he had organised lunch for them at the Market Hotel. This was not a hotel in the European sense but a large restaurant reached by a staircase rising from the fish market where rows of skipjack tuna, yellowfin and frigate mackerel were laid out on concrete slabs.

The restaurant was packed with men and youths, but there were no women present, and the entrance of three foreign females caused much turning of heads and staring. But the interest they aroused was curious rather than lecherous.

A large table with a view of the harbour was ready for them, spread with bowls of rice, several curries, poppadoms, sliced tomatoes and onions, grated coconut and *roshi*, the pancake-like bread of the islands.

Manik and the two boatmen ate with them, and for Charlotte it was the best meal of the trip. Real island food, one of the curries palate-searingly hot and all of them more authentic than the tourist food served on board.

The others, except Dean, found the food a bit too spicy and peppery. He tried everything and had some second helpings. From time to time, as dishes were passed back and forth across the table, Charlotte met his eyes and wondered if he had had as little sleep as she.

She was still no closer to a decision than she had been last night before supper. But time was running out. Very soon she must make up her mind one way or the other.

Part of her longed to go with him and experience the bliss of which yesterday afternoon in her cabin had been a foretaste. But the sensible side of her nature still counselled caution. And she could not help worrying about the effect on Manik if Dean told him he was leaving and taking her with him.

If Manik did care for her, she could not bear to hurt him.

CHAPTER TEN

'THERE seems to be a lot of the main course left,' Janet said worriedly, as bowls of tinned fruit were brought to their table.

'Don't worry. The food we haven't eaten will be left out and the empty bowls replenished for the next customers. We shall only be charged for what we've had,' Charlotte told her.

'Really? How did you know that?' asked Janet.

'Charlotte's grandfather lived here,' said Dean, from across the table. 'She can probably tell you what those are,' indicating small dishes of finely sliced nuts.

'They're the nuts of the areca palm. Maldivians like to nibble them after eating, but I think they're a taste you have to acquire in childhood.' Charlotte looked at her watch. Then, leaning towards him, she said, 'If you'll excuse me, Manik, I'd like to look round the new mosque before the afternoon prayers.'

'We'll meet here at four... no later,' he said, glancing out of the window at the still white-flecked sea beyond the wall of the harbour.

She nodded and left the table, relieved that, although he rose to his feet, Dean made no attempt to follow her. The others had already said they didn't want to see the mosque, and perhaps he shared their lack of interest. Or perhaps he sensed that she hadn't made her decision yet.

She knew that the mosque would be closed to non-Muslims for fifteen minutes before prayers and an hour afterwards, so this was a good time to go. Although, had she been unsuitably dressed, she would not have been admitted. But her decorous white blouse and long dark culottes, and her fluent Dhivehi, made her an acceptable visitor. After removing her shoes and washing her feet, she was shown the great hall with its carved wooden doors and panelling where six thousand people could pray; and also the rest of the complex, including a conference hall, a library and classrooms.

Dean was waiting for her when she walked down the impressively wide flight of steps in front of the building. As soon she saw him standing there, she knew what her answer must be.

If they were meant for each other, it would come right in the end. But in spite of what had happened in her cabin, there were two reasons why she could not spend an unofficial honeymoon with him.

The reason she would tell him was that she couldn't hurt Manik. The reason she would keep to herself was that she had to be sure Dean loved her. If she knew that, she would follow him to the ends of the earth.

'There's a small park across the street where we could sit in the shade,' he said, as she joined him. 'Have you decided?'

She nodded. 'I'm sorry, Dean. I can't come with you. Mainly because of Manik. I think I'm probably going to have to hurt him quite a lot before the voyage is over, but to go off with you would be unnecessarily cruel.'

He received her decision in silence. They had passed through the gates of the park, once part of the grounds of the sultans' palace, and were walking slowly along the main path before he spoke.

At last he said, 'I rang London this morning...I wanted to check with my office that a project was progressing smoothly. It is, but my mother is laid up. She's had a fall and hurt her back. It may not to be serious and she gave instructions that I was not to be told, but my secretary thought I should know. I'm flying back tonight. So what I suggested last night has fallen through anyway.'

'I see.' What she saw was that if only he had told her his news before asking for her decision, she might have been able to avoid rejecting his proposition. 'I'm sorry about your mother. How did it happen?'

'They've been having a cold snap in England, and she slipped on some icy steps. It only happened yesterday.' He put a hand on her shoulder and turned her to face him. 'If I couldn't persuade you to share a Maldivian idyll, I suppose I'd be wasting my breath if I asked you to forgo the rest of your holiday and fly back to sub-zero London with me?'

'I'm afraid you would, but not because I'd mind giving up the holiday, or because of the weather in England,' Charlotte told him.

'Don't tell me. Let me guess...Manik wouldn't like it,' he said sardonically.

'This has nothing to do with Manik. I'm not going back to England with the others next Sunday. I'm staying here...to work. I told you I'd been a travel courier. Now I've been appointed manager of a resort island. Not in Kaafu Atoll—further south. I'm due to start there next Monday. I have to be there, my employers are depending on me.'

'Which of the tour operators do you work for?' he asked.

She told him. 'But they've been bought out by Jardine Latimer. Not that the take-over should affect me. I've been on the pay-roll a long time and I have a good record.'

'I'm sure you have. So you're likely to be in the Maldives for some time?'

'Indefinitely...that was the plan. But plans do change...as yours have.'

Dean released his hold on her shoulder and thrust his hands into his pockets. He was frowning.

'We seem to be in a deadlock. You have to stay; I have to go. Apart from my mother's accident, I have a lot of commitments in the next few weeks. It looks as if the gods, having brought us together, have decided to keep us apart.'

'It looks like it,' she agreed. And suddenly her throat was tight and there were tears prickling her eyelids. She turned away, pretending to examine a shrub.

'How was the mosque, love?' Vic's now familiar voice rang out from somewhere nearby.

Hastily pulling herself together, Charlotte turned towards one of the side paths and, as he and Olly came closer, said, 'Very interesting.' To her relief her voice didn't quaver.

'Where did they get the money to build it, that's what I'd like to know,' said Vic. 'I thought they were supposed to be hard up. They don't get that many tourists.'

'They were helped by the Gulf States and Brunei. Did you enjoy the museum?'

'Janet and Bill seem to like it. They're still in there,' Olly told her. 'But there's nothing much to see. Some fancy dress outfits worn by the sultans with the gold embroidery all tarnished. Old stuff like that gives me the creeps. We're going back to the café we found this morning to have an ice cream. How about you two?'

'We're on our way to the museum,' said Dean. 'See you later.'

On their way in, they met Dr and Mrs Warren coming out.

'You'll be shadowed by an attendant all the way round, but there are some interesting things,' Janet told them. 'The trouble is not much is labelled. Don't miss the embroidered silk envelopes for official letters to the sultans.'

The museum was on two floors, with stairs as steep as companionways rising to the upper floor.

'What time do you have to leave for the airport?' Charlotte asked, as they walked round the glass cases containing the exhibits.

'About four-thirty. Manik is arranging for a launch to pick me up before you sail to Kuda Bandos. It won't take me more than ten minutes to pack my kit. I can have a shower at the airport, I'm told.'

Charlotte felt as if she had been kicked in the stomach. She couldn't believe that in an hour they would be saying goodbye...perhaps forever.

Dean said to the Maldivian girl who was following them round, 'Do you speak English?'

She shook her head apologetically.

He turned to Charlotte. 'If I give you my address, will you write to me?'

'If you'll write to me.'

'Of course.' He glanced at the attendant. 'Is there any way to get rid of her? I want to kiss you goodbye. Would a fat tip do the trick?'

'I doubt it, but I may be able to persuade her.' She turned to the girl and said in Dhivehi, 'I have given my heart to this man, but his mother is ill and he must go back to Europe. He is leaving for the airport soon. We want to be alone for a few minutes. I promise we won't steal or damage anything.' Seeing the girl looking doubtful, she added, 'I may not see him for months...perhaps never again. I must feel his arms round me once more. Please be kind to us!'

The girl nodded. 'I know how you feel. My friend loved a man who was in political trouble and was banished to another atoll. That was more than a year ago, and she is still very unhappy. I will leave you with your man.'

'What did you say to her?' asked Dean, when she had gone.

'Only that we wanted to say goodbye in private. One of her friends has a boyfriend who was banished. That's the usual punishment here for most forms of wrong-doing. Often the men don't mind being sent away, but it's hard on their girlfriends and wives.'

Dean took hold of her hands and drew her towards him. 'I find it very hard to leave you. But there's an Italian saying "*che sará, sará*"—what will be, will be. I don't think it will be too long before we meet again.'

It was not what she wanted to hear. Not, I love you, Charlotte. I'll be back. Or, Chuck your job, and as soon as you've worked out your notice, come back to England and marry me.

Aloud, she said, 'Don't you? Well...who knows?'

He pulled her against him, but not to kiss her. Instead of tilting her head back, as he had yesterday, he held her as if she were a child in need of comfort, his embrace more protective than passionate.

With her face hidden against his shoulder, Charlotte felt the tears she had controlled in the garden well up and seep through her tightly closed eyelids.

Dean felt the convulsive breaths she was trying not to let become sobs.

'Don't cry...there's no need to cry.'

'I know. It's stupid of me.' With an enormous effort, she forced herself to stop. 'I can't think why I'm being so emotional. I don't make a habit of it.'

'Maybe that's why,' he said gently.

'What do you mean?'

'People who bottle things up get to a point when the cork has to pop. As it did, in a different way, yesterday.' He put one hand under her chin and made her look up at him. 'You surprised me. I thought, when we started this trip, it would take a long time and a lot of gentle persuasion to get you to let yourself go. But it didn't, did it? Not much on the beach at Boduhithi, and even less in your cabin.'

The amusement in his eyes made a fiery blush sweep from her throat to her forehead.

Then he bent his head to kiss her, and all the divine sensations she had felt in his arms yesterday revived and made her forget everything but the joy of being held in strong arms and knowing that he wanted her.

They stayed so long in the museum that they had to run to the meeting place, watched with surprise by the locals who, like most people in hot climates, rarely did more than amble.

But only Manik noticed that they were a few minutes late and that Charlotte was out of breath. The others were much more interested in the fact that Diane had induced the Professor to have his beard shaved off and had also persuaded him to buy several carriers of new clothes. He was wearing some of them: a vividly patterned shirt and a pair of white trousers. Charlotte would have passed him in the street and not recognised him.

The wind was still fresh-to-strong, and everyone in the dinghy got very wet on the way back to the schooner.

Getting Diane to grab the ladder at the right moment was even harder than getting her to let go of it earlier. But to Manik's visible relief, the possibility of someone being injured by stepping on to a low rung and having a heel or calf bashed by the side of the dinghy as it bucked about on the turbulent water did not materialise. Everyone was put aboard safely.

Less than half an hour later, Charlotte watched Dean drop his rollbag into the well of the launch which would take him to Hulhule, the island near Malé where the jets landed.

Their final farewell was typically British; a handshake accompanied by a social peck on the cheek from him and a bright smile from her.

'What a shame,' said Olly sympathetically, as they stood by the rails, waving to him. 'He was nice. You got on well, didn't you? Still, there's always more fish in the sea for a girl with your looks... and you don't have to look too far neither,' with a meaning nudge.

Had she been alone, Charlotte would have watched the launch until it was lost to view. But with the others there, and feeling Manik's eyes on her, she was one of the first to turn away. She didn't want anyone to guess that, inwardly, she felt as anguished as the day they had broken the news that her grandfather was dead.

A fortnight earlier Charlotte wouldn't have believed that at her age she was still capable of spending the whole night soaking her pillow with tears like a young girl in love for the first time.

In the morning her eyelids were puffy and she felt exhausted. But fortunately this wasn't noticed, because both Bill and Olly had been stricken by a tummy bug and their partners were too busy ministering to them to pay attention to her.

'Bill makes an appalling patient. Most doctors do,' Janet told her.

Vic said, 'It must have been something Ol ate at that restaurant yesterday. I didn't think much of the place, and God knows what the kitchens were like.'

Charlotte surmised that the kitchens were probably no less hygienic than most restaurant kitchens in Europe, but she kept this opinion to herself. The ices both couples had eaten were a more likely source of infection than any local food.

She spent most of the day snorkelling outside the reef which encircled Kuda Bandos, a small island kept as a nature reserve.

By late afternoon Bill and Olly were feeling better, although they remained on deck reading while Vic and Janet had a swim.

While Vic was snorkelling and she was sitting on the beach with Charlotte, the doctor's wife said, 'I'm amazed by the transformation Diane's wrought in the Prof— Paddy, as she calls him. Without that horrid beard, he looks quite presentable. She's even making him take proper showers twice a day. Do you think they're having it off, as the young say? I should have thought it was nearly impossible in a narrow bunk with next to no headroom, but perhaps that's a middle-aged view.'

'I don't know, but, if they are, can it work out?' asked Charlotte. 'I mean, will it end at Heathrow, or will it go on, do you think?'

'Who can say with these holiday affairs? The Professor does need a woman to take him in hand, but I can't see Diane fitting in with the other dons' wives if he should be mad enough to marry her. But perhaps it might not be madness if she makes him happy and comfortable,' Janet went on thoughtfully. 'Most of the old class-divisions have broken down. Perhaps his colleagues might regard it as a piece of amusing eccentricity. And who knows? Diane may have the capacity, given some private tutorials, to develop into an intelligent woman.'

'It's possible,' Charlotte agreed, wondering if Janet guessed that she herself had fallen for Dean.

As if reading her mind, the other woman said, 'It's a pity Dean had to cut short his holiday—I liked him very much. Did he tell you much about himself? What his profession is?'

'No, he didn't.'

'Bill thinks he might be in the Special Air Services and that's why he never mentioned his occupation. The SAS are notoriously secretive, and it's fairly unusual for a man in his thirties to be as fit as Dean is. We felt he was a very tough nut, but perhaps that was just our impression. He was always friendly, with very nice manners, but there was something...' a pause to choose the right word '...something *steely* about him. An iron hand in a velvet glove.'

'I thought so too,' agreed Charlotte.

She wondered if Janet suspected that something had happened and was waiting for her to confide in her. But Charlotte had never confided her troubles to anyone. She had been Kay's and Sally's confidante, but had kept her own problems to her self.

And what was there to confide? Only that she had given her heart to a man who had asked her to write to him but, in a somewhat hurried departure, had forgotten to leave his address.

She could find it out easily enough. It would be on the computer at head office, because all the company's customers had the new brochures mailed to them. But she wouldn't make the enquiry. She would wait for him to write to her. Any man with initiative could easily discover how to make contact with her. If he wanted to.

On the last day of the cruise, Charlotte said goodbye to the others soon after breakfast. She was taking a seaplane to Fadippolu Atoll, far to the south. They would be leaving on the evening flight to London.

To explain why she wasn't going back with them, she had to tell them about her new job.

'Some people have all the luck!' Olly said enviously. 'It'll be months before any of us see the sun again. I'm not looking forward to going back to work, I can tell you.'

'Nor me!' agreed Vic, with a grimace. 'This sea air suits my lungs a lot better than sitting in traffic jams all day.'

'There's a big difference between being on holiday and working here,' Charlotte said drily. 'I shan't be doing a lot of sunbathing.'

Little did any of them know how much she longed to be going back to the winter-bound city which, in spite of all its drawbacks, was now—because Dean was there—the place where her heart was.

'You'll keep in touch, love, won't you?' Olly said, as they exchanged a final hugs.

'Of course,' said Charlotte.

But she knew how seldom holiday friendships lasted. They were as ephemeral as holiday romances. Unless people happened to live close to each other, or had some strong common interest, relationships forged in surroundings such as the Maldives, with everyone relaxed and at leisure, rarely survived the pressures of day-to-day life once the holidaymakers returned to their normal environments.

'Goodbye, my dear. Do look us up if ever you're in the area,' Janet said warmly.

'All the best, love. Don't do anything I wouldn't do,' Diane giggled.

Bill and the Professor shook hands, but Vic kissed her on both cheeks.

'You're a smasher, Charlie,' he said, reminding her of Stanley Neasden's annoyance when Vic had called him Stan before dinner on the first night of the cruise. Was it really only two weeks since that evening? Somehow it seemed far longer.

Stanley and Sylvia were still on Bandos. They would be rejoining the group at the airport later.

'I feel the same way about you, Vic. Olly's a very lucky lady,' Charlotte told him sincerely.

Then she shook hands and said goodbye to Maumoon, Hassan and Ali before, for the last time, climbing down to the launch where Manik was waiting to take her to the Inter Atoll Air depot.

Waving and calling goodbye, the others watched the launch zoom away from the schooner, Olly seizing the opportunity for another snapshot on the last of the many reels of film the Parsons had used to record all the main events of their holiday.

Charlotte kept her eyes on *Sea Bird* until the people aboard her were reduced to indistinguishable specks. Now there was only one more person to say goodbye to—Manik.

She had expected Maumoon to see her off. When she realised the boatman was staying on board and Manik was taking her, she concluded he must want to speak to her privately. But it seemed she was mistaken. He carried her baggage from the launch to the check-in without saying anything more personal than, 'Perhaps, when I have my leave, I will come to see you. But that will not be for some months.'

When they shook hands he did hold her palm in his for longer than was necessary, and there was a look in his eyes suggesting he would like to say more. But, whatever was on his mind, he kept to himself.

'*A-salam alekum.*' It could mean hello or farewell.

'Goodbye, Manik. Take care of yourself.'

She watched him walk briskly away, their parting causing her pain, but not the same deep sense of loss she had felt when Dean said goodbye.

Two weeks later, when she had begun to despair, a letter came through on the fax machine.

It came from a village in Dorset and was signed 'Dean.' It asked how she was, told her his mother had recovered, said he had been very busy. No amount of wishful thinking could make it a love letter.

Her reply was equally non-committal, mainly about her new job and the challenges it presented. She was particularly anxious to improve the food offered to visitors by using hydroponics to grow vegetables for salads.

She had been in her new post a month before she took a day off to go to Malé.

There, an enquiry at the *poste restante* counter at the Post Office produced two envelopes addressed to her. One was from Janet, the other from Olly. Both contained prints of their holiday snaps. Three shots included Dean.

Her next call was to the Mohamed Ismail Didi private library where her grandfather had spent many hours reading old copies of the *National Geographic* and other periodicals, and to which he had bequeathed his own library. As she had hoped, among his books was a collected edition of the work of the Victorian poet Swinburne.

It did not include the lines Dean had quoted to her, but she found them at the back of the book in a poem called 'Love and Sleep' which her grandfather must have copied from another source.

She made a copy of his copy and that night, alone in her room, she looked at the pictures of Dean and re-read the second verse.

And all her face was honey to my mouth.
    And all her body pasture to mine eyes;
        The long lithe arms and hotter hands than fire,
The quivering flanks, hair smelling of the south.
        The bright light feet, the splendid supple thighs
            And glittering eyelids of my soul's desire.

It was clear now why *Love and Sleep* had not been printed in the collected edition her grandfather had received as a prize at school soon after the first world war. In those days the poem would have been thought shockingly erotic.

No longer shocking, it was still erotic, especially when read with a vivid memory of Dean's visit to her cabin. Every moment of the day and night when she wasn't asleep or concentrating on her work, Charlotte longed for him.

One morning, not long after sunrise, she went for a walk round the island, and suddenly, out of the sea, came a line of footprints.

Having grown up on an island where everyone went barefoot, including her grandfather, she had learnt to recognise familiar footprints as easily as people elsewhere recognised a friend's handwriting. The prints on the beach ahead of her were exactly like Dean's; the instep clearly defined, the outline that of a man who from childhood had worn well-made shoes—the toes less splayed than Manik's—and who had a long easy stride.

Filled with wild excitement at the thought that Dean had come back, she followed the prints, breaking into a run in the hope of catching him up. Until she came to a place where the footprints stopped and there were marks on the sand which a tourist might not have recognised for what they were; the marks of a devout Muslim, kneeling with his head towards Mecca and, as dawn broke over the sea, performing the first of the day's five devotions.

Most Maldivians said these early prayers in their houses, after washing with water from their well. But the man whose prints she had followed must have cleansed himself in the sea before choosing this secluded spot for his prayers.

It was likely that he was one of the Bangladeshi waiters working on the island. Sure enough, when they went on from the place where he had prayed, the footprints turned off at a ride cut through the island's vegetation and leading to the staff quarters.

As she continued her walk, Charlotte realised that the hope that Dean had come back had been a crazy flight of imagination. Far from returning to the islands, it was likely that, in his own environment, he would soon forget her. England was a long, long way from the middle of the Indian Ocean.

A few days later she had a surprise visit from Manik.

'What are you doing here? You haven't lost your job, have you?' she asked, remembering his anxiety that there might be repercussions from Sylvia Neasden's accident.

'No, I have left Maumoon in charge. He knows what he's doing, in fact he will probably replace me when I start my new job.'

'What new job is this?' asked Charlotte, opening the small refrigerator in the corner of her office to get out a cold drink for him. It was late afternoon and although, as the resort's manager, she was on call at all hours of the day and night, she had already dealt with the day's routine work.

'I am to have a new schooner and a share of the profits,' he told her proudly.

'Manik, that's wonderful! When did this happen?'

'You remember you said you would help me write to the head of the company which has bought out the operators who are chartering *Sea Bird*? They have written to me. Look, this is the letter.'

He produced a piece of paper, unfolded it and offered it to her.

Under Jardine Latimer's letterheading, their Special Projects Manager had written to offer Manik the command of a luxury schooner with berths for twenty passengers.

'It has been reported to us by a close friend of the chairman that you have both the professional and personal qualifications needed for this highly responsible position within our organisation. The terms of your contract would include...'

When Charlotte had finished reading, she said, 'The chairman's close friend has to be Dean Richmond.'

Manik frowned. 'I don't agree. I think it was Professor Paddington.'

'I suppose that's possible,' she said doubtfully. 'Or it might have been Bill Warren. He might be the chairman's GP.'

'GP? What is GP?' he queried.

Charlotte explained that it stood for general practitioner, the doctor whom people in Britain consulted for all their minor ailments.

'But it doesn't really matter who recommended you, does it? The important thing is that it's a much better deal than the one you've got at the moment. I'm terribly pleased for you, Manik. It's what you deserve. You are a *very* good skipper.'

They had dinner together in the island's restaurant, which was built out over the lagoon and thatched with palm. Charlotte saw several of the women tourists looking with curiosity and perhaps envy at her handsome companion.

After dinner Manik suggested a walk along the moonlit beach. Instinct warned her it would be better to avoid being completely alone with him, but she couldn't think of an excuse which he wouldn't see through and be offended by.

'As long as we don't go beyond where I can be seen. I'm supposed to be on call at all times, except on my days off,' she told him.

Tonight, with a full moon shining, the beach to the south of the restaurant looked like a picture on the cover of a travel brochure. The sand was as white as icing sugar, the palms bent gracefully over the glittering lagoon and a line of surf showed where the ocean began.

They left their shoes under a bush and Manik turned up the bottoms of his trousers. He was wearing a *Sea Bird* T-shirt, white with the outline of a schooner printed across his chest.

'When do you have to go back?' asked Charlotte. As they had when they were children, they had been speaking Dhivehi ever since he arrived.

'Tomorrow. I cannot stay more than one night. But I had to tell you my news because now, at last, I can say what is in my heart. Before that was not possible. I did not have enough to offer a woman like you, my beloved.'

She knew there was no way to stop Manik declaring himself. All she could do was listen and try to be as gentle as possible when he allowed her to speak.

'It can't surprise you to learn that I love you, Charlotte... that I want you to be my wife, the mother of my sons. We can make a good life together. I don't want a wife who stays at home while I go to sea. I want to have my woman with me. On the new schooner there will be comfortable quarters and you will enjoy meeting and talking to the passengers. You will not be cut off from Europeans.'

He slipped an arm round her waist and drew her against him. 'But these are practical matters, and on a night such as this, with a woman as beautiful as you, it is better to kiss than to talk.'

Last time he had kissed her by force. This time his embrace was gentle and Charlotte was able, by pressing her hands against his chest, to stop him from kissing her.

'Dear Manik, I'm very fond of you, but my fondness is that of a sister... not of a wife. I can never love you in the way you deserve. My heart belongs to another...'

* * *

For days after Manik had gone, Charlotte wondered if she had rejected a good man, and a way of life which could have been happy and contented, for a love which, like a mirage, must remain forever out of reach.

She was tormented by memories of things Dean had said which could be construed in an unpleasant way, such as, 'You surprised me. I thought, when we started this trip, that it would take a long time and a lot of gentle persuasion to get you to let yourself go. But it didn't, did it? Not much on the beach at Boduhithi, and even less in your cabin.'

If she hadn't been blinded by love, would she have recognised that remark as a sign that he was an experienced seducer?

But he had also said, 'I find it very hard to leave you,' and told her that he had a lot of commitments ahead of him.

Although the address on his letter—Mill Cottage, Long Lane—suggested a rural retreat, there had been a fax number as well as a telephone number.

Charlotte decided to fax a reply to his letter. Manik had given her a reason for writing, and if Dean *had* been the instrument of Manik's good fortune he deserved to be thanked.

She wrote several drafts before she was satisfied with:

Dear Dean,

I've had an unexpected visit from Manik. He's been offered the command of a new schooner on a profit-sharing basis. I suspect that you are 'the friend of Jardine Latimer's chairman' who put in a good word for him. If so, it was an act of great kindness for which, being very fond of Manik, I am deeply grateful to you.

When he came to tell me his good news, he also asked me to marry him. But on my side the affection is sisterly. I hated having to turn him down, but I'm sure he will find the right girl for him eventually. He's a super guy, but not—to misquote Walt Whitman—the man who waits for me.

Otherwise there's not much news. The job is interesting and every day is different, but at times I feel restless. When I lived here before, I wasn't conscious of how far from the rest of the world these islands are. Now I am.

My grandfather used to sing an old song which began: How're you going to keep 'em down on the farm after they've seen Paree?

That's rather the way I feel.

Charlotte

She faxed the letter on a Friday, hoping Dean would be at the cottage the following day or on Sunday, but knowing that he might not go down to Dorset every weekend, especially when the weather was bad.

It might even be several weeks before he saw the letter, unless he had some arrangement whereby letters and faxes to the cottage were redirected to his London pad.

The following Tuesday she received a message from her new masters.

Typed in peremptory capitals and phrased in the terse style of an old-fashioned cablegram, it was signed by the manager of Jardine Latimer's head office.

YOUR PRESENCE REQUIRED HERE IMMEDIATELY. PLEASE BE READY TO LEAVE AS SOON AS YOUR REPLACEMENT ARRIVES.

With mounting bewilderment, mingled with consternation, Charlotte read her replacement's flight details and realised that she was expected to fly out later that day; not on the evening charter flight taking a group of her tourists back to Europe, but on an earlier scheduled flight.

It was no use sending a fax asking for an explanation. In England everyone but night workers would be asleep. By the time head office opened at nine o'clock UK time, her replacement would have landed at Malé and she would have learned from him the reason for this arbitrary summons to London.

CHAPTER ELEVEN

HIS name was Bob Temple, and he was the first to come through Customs to where Charlotte was waiting to meet him.

But, after they had shaken hands and she had controlled her curiosity long enough to make polite enquiries about his journey, she found that he could not enlighten her.

'I have no idea what it's all about,' he said. 'I only know there's a big shake-up going on, and the likes of us had better do as we're told or we could find ourselves redundant. The new boss is a hard man, I hear... a real old-fashioned despot. Anyone who doesn't like the way he runs things doesn't last long. And, to give the devil his due, the way he runs things has proved extremely successful.'

There was another surprise awaiting Charlotte when Bob handed over the air ticket he had brought for her. The flight she was booked on had a First Class section, and she was to travel in that class with all its superior comforts.

Bob had also brought her a letter containing some further instructions. She was to report to an interview at Head Office at five o'clock the following afternoon. This would at least give her time to bathe, change and—depending on how well she slept on the flight—either take a nap or, London weather permitting, some exercise before facing whatever ordeal might lie ahead of her.

* * *

When Charlotte emerged into the public concourse at Heathrow the following morning, bracing herself for a chilly wait for the airbus which would take her close to her London base, one of the drivers awaiting passengers with private transport laid on was holding a placard with her surname on it.

Thinking there must be someone else with the same name coming through—flights from all parts of the world landed at Heathrow every few minutes—she would have ignored the placard. But the man holding it intercepted her.

'Are you Miss Charlotte Perivale, miss?'

'Yes... but how did you know?'

'I was shown a picture of you, miss,' he said, taking charge of her baggage.

Charlotte's eyebrows rose even higher. 'Really? By whom?'

'By my boss, miss. He was given it by the firm you work for, Jardine Latimer. I'm to take you to your home address and pick you up again at half past four this afternoon.'

To have a taxi awaiting her threw Charlotte into even deeper perplexity.

As they drove away from the terminal, the driver opened the glass partition behind his seat and said, 'If you don't mind me saying so, miss, you look a very young lady to be a VIP... which I assume you are, like most of the gents I fetch and take to the airport.'

Charlotte laughed. 'Sorry to disappoint you, but I'm no VIP. Far from it! Why I'm getting preferential treatment is a mystery to me. But I must say it's very pleasant to be in a warm taxi instead of stamping my feet at the airbus stop, which is what I expected to do.'

'You've got a lovely tan. Been somewhere nice?' he asked.

Had she come back by charter flight, the last thing she would have wanted was to be questioned by an inquisitive cab-driver. But having had an excellent dinner followed by six hours' sleep and a delicious breakfast, she was glad to chat to keep her mind off this afternoon's appointment.

She told the driver a little about the Maldives and about meeting one of his colleagues there. No doubt by now Vic and Olly had lost their holiday tans, she thought. An artificially brown skin didn't last long in this climate.

It wasn't raining at the moment, but there had been heavy rain during the night or yesterday. The sky was still an unbroken mass of grey clouds and the fields between the airport and outer London had a bleak, sodden look which was doubly depressing to eyes accustomed to the bright light and glittering waters of the Indian Ocean.

When the cab-driver returned for her later that day, Charlotte was waiting for him in a smart suit belonging to Sally. She had telephoned her flatmate at the Press Association for permission to borrow something suitable for an interview on which her future might depend.

Sally owned a lot of smart, expensive clothes, and at her suggestion Charlotte was wearing an almost new camel gabardine jacket and skirt with a printed silk shirt. With her tan, and her sun-streaked hair, the effect was subtle and sophisticated. At Sally's insistence, she had also borrowed the shoes and bag her friend had bought for the outfit. Both were a lovely shade of caramel, the shoes Italian, the bag French, lined with matching suede and with its maker's name on a small gilt-metal label above the zipped inside pocket.

Charlotte, who never had occasion to buy and wear clothes and accessories of this quality, felt that now, thanks to Sally's generosity, she did look as if she might be a VIP, if only a minor one.

The driver gave an added boost to her self-confidence when, having jumped out to open the passenger door for her, he said, 'My word, you look a knock-out in that outfit, miss! It's not often I see a young lady got up as smart as paint these days. It seems to be more the fashion to look as if they've slept rough. And don't take me wrong, but you smell as good as you look. That's a real nice perfume. French, is it?'

Charlotte had used one of Kay's many sprays, knowing her friend wouldn't mind as she always had more bottles of scent than she could use before their contents lost their freshness.

As the taxi took her to her destination, Charlotte hoped that whoever had summoned her would endorse the driver's approval. Not knowing whom she was to see, or why, made her nervous.

The Jardine Latimer head office was one of the oldest houses in Berkeley Square. It was six minutes to five when Charlotte entered the building, and saw with approval that the interior retained its dignified panelling and an elegant black and white marble floor. The receptionist's desk was an antique, and the flowers on it and elsewhere were fresh and arranged naturally, not stiffly.

The grey-haired, elegant receptionist said, 'Good afternoon, Miss Perivale. If you'd like to sit down for a moment, I'll get someone to take you upstairs.'

'Who shall I be seeing?' asked Charlotte 'The personnel manager?'

The older woman showed a hint of surprise. 'You're seeing Mr Latimer himself.' It was said in the tone in which an official at Buckingham Palace might have said, 'You're seeing Her Majesty the Queen,' or someone at the Vatican, 'You're seeing His Holiness the Pope.'

'I—I see.'

Charlotte sat down on the chair indicated and tried to steady her nerves with some discreet deep breathing.

Presently another middle-aged woman appeared and said, 'Will you come this way, please, Miss Perivale?'

She was led up the wide Turkey-carpeted staircase to the first floor landing and from there to an ante-room arranged as a secretary's office. The woman picked up an internal telephone and, when a voice answered, said, 'Miss Perivale is here, Mr Latimer. Yes, sir.'

Replacing the receiver, she made a beckoning motion to Charlotte before opening the heavy mahogany door between the office and the inner room.

'Miss Perivale,' she announced, standing aside for Charlotte to enter and confront the formidable-sounding Mr Latimer.

But it wasn't the beetle-browed, flint-eyed man in his fifties whom Charlotte had expected to face who rose from behind a large partners' desk and came round it to offer his hand.

'Hello, Charlotte,' said Dean, smiling down at her. 'How was your flight? Rather more comfortable than our flight to Malé, I hope?'

It was automatic to shake hands. As soon as his fingers closed over hers, every nerve in her body quivered, But she managed to answer with more composure than she felt, 'Very comfortable, thank you.' Then her bewilderment broke through. 'Did *you* arrange that? For me to travel First Class?'

He nodded. 'I didn't want you to be jet-lagged. Important decisions should never be made in a state of fatigue.'

'What important decisions?' she queried.

'We'll come to that later. First I want to apologise for misleading you. As you now realise, Richmond is not my surname, but it is my second name. It was my

mother's maiden name. She uses it for professional pur-
poses and I use it when I'm travelling incognito. Like
my father and grandfather, I make a point of testing the
holidays Jardine Latimer sell.'

'*You* are Jardine Latimer!' She hadn't quite taken that
in.

'That's right. But I've always been called Dean to dis-
tinguish me from my father.'

There was a tap at the door and a woman in a navy
blue overall came in with a tea tray, which she carried
to a tripod table by one of the two wing chairs on either
side of the fire.

'Thank you, Mrs Hendon. Will you sit here,
Charlotte?' Dean indicated the chair opposite the one
where the tray had been placed. 'I think I'd better pour
out while you recover from the shock of finding that
your new employer is someone you already know fairly
well.'

The amused glance he gave her behind his tea-lady's
back was an effective reminder of how far beyond the
professional their relationship had gone when she had
no idea of his true identity.

But after Mrs Hendon had left the room, his manner
reverted to that of a courteous host.

'You'll be pleased to hear that some mild, dry weather
is forecast for the rest of the week. You wouldn't have
liked the sleet we had last weekend.'

'No,' said Charlotte, looking gratefully at the log fire.
At the flat the heating was controlled by a time clock
and had been off while she was there. But this building
was warm everywhere, and especially here, close to a
crackling fire; a real one, not an imitation, with a basket
of wood beside it.

'This is very civilised,' she said. 'More like a private
drawing-room than the office of a tycoon.'

'God forbid that I should ever become a tycoon in the pejorative sense in which that term is usually applied,' he answered. 'This room reflects the tastes of several generations of Latimers, all of them highly civilised. Some people would dispute my claim to being like them. It's a rough world we live in, and sometimes I have to use more Draconian methods than my predecessors.' He paused. 'I'm sure your grandfather told you about Draco, the famous law-maker of seventh-century Athens, whose name is still associated with rigorous punishment for wrongdoing.'

Charlotte said, 'Yes, but if you're sometimes severe, I'm sure you're never unjust. A latter-day Draco wouldn't have done all the kind things you did for the Neasdens, or arranged for me to fly First and be met by a taxi.'

'My treatment of the Neasdens was in line with company policy. You——' He broke off to bring her a cup of tea and a silver milk jug. 'You are a special case,' he finished, placing them on the table at her elbow.

'I am?' said Charlotte. 'Why is that?'

Dean chose to ignore the question. 'Have you had any lunch?' he asked.

'An apple. I had a good breakfast, but I was too keyed up to feel hungry at lunchtime. It's quite disturbing, you know, to be summoned at very short notice from the other side of the world...well, if not quite the other side, from a long way away. Why *did* you send for me?' she finished.

'Drink your tea and have something to eat.' He brought her a plate with a small linen napkin on it and a larger dish of the elegant sandwiches served in expensive hotels. 'Take two or three—they're very small.'

She did as she was told. Clearly he would come to the point of this interview at a moment of his own choosing. He was not to be hurried.

When he had seated himself in the other chair, he said, 'I wasn't expecting you to look quite so soignée. This elegant new persona—at least, new to me—must turn a lot of heads, but I think I prefer you when you have sand in your toes.'

'You look rather different yourself,' she pointed out.

Today he was dressed in the finely striped navy blue worsted of the boardroom, the gentlemen's club and other exclusive enclaves frequented by men of affairs. But inside the expensive, expertly tailored cloth was the strong virile body she remembered in disturbing detail.

And if she could see in her mind's eye all the long, powerful, sun-tanned length of him, so he must be able to visualise the flesh concealed by Sally's silk shirt and suit.

'I suppose I do,' he conceded. 'This——' with a sweeping gesture which included everything he wore from the conservative silk tie to the gleaming black calf shoes, probably hand-made '—is not how I choose to dress. But it's the appropriate rig for the meetings I've had to attend today. Will you have dinner with me?'

The question was as unexpected as most of the things which had happened since yesterday morning.

'Do I have any choice?' she asked.

Dean arched a dark eyebrow. 'What are you suggesting? That I'd use my position as head of the firm you work for to pressure you into dining with me . . . and perhaps to extract other favours?'

'No, not really . . . although it has been known.'

'I'm sure it has, but you're quite free to refuse if you have other plans for the evening,' said Dean.

'No one knows I'm here . . . except Sally, one of my flatmates,' Charlotte told him. 'I rang her to say I was back, although I wasn't able to tell her for how long.'

'That depends on a number of things. By the way, thank you for your last letter. It sounds as if you aren't enjoying being back in the islands as much as you expected to. Why is that?'

The truthful answer was: Because I met you, and that changed everything.

What she said was, 'The Maldives are different . . . I'm different.' She left it at that. 'I'd like to have dinner with you. Sally won't mind—she has a date this evening. I think I should ring and tell her I'm also going to be out. She'll be expecting me to be there when she goes home to change.'

'Call her now,' he suggested. 'What's her surname and office number?'

Charlotte told him, and was slightly surprised when he dialled the number himself. While the Press Association switchboard operator was putting the call through, he beckoned Charlotte to come to his desk where he was sitting on its front edge in the posture of a man on a shooting stick.

A moment after he handed over the receiver, Sally came on the line.

'Sally, this is Charlotte. I'm just calling to say that I'll be out this evening.' She was conscious that Dean hadn't gone back to the fire but was still close by, watching her.

'Where are you?' Her friend sounded puzzled. 'I thought your appointment at HQ was at five.'

'It was. That's where I am . . . in Jardine Latimer's office. I'll explain later. I expect I'll be home before you——' Dean signalled that she wouldn't '—but, in case I'm not, I thought I ought to call you. See you later. 'Bye!'

As she replaced the receiver, Dean put both hands on her waist.

'I wasn't going to do this yet, but I can't keep my hands off you. Let's get straight to the point. Have you missed me as much as I've missed you?'

As he spoke he spread his knees and drew her between them until they were a foot apart and the natural place to put her hands was against his chest.

Trembling inwardly, she said, 'I didn't know you had missed me.'

'Intolerably! Every hour of every day since I last had you in my arms at the museum. Kiss me.'

Suddenly, all the doubts of the past weeks evaporated. She smiled into his eyes, which for once were on a level with hers. 'Is that an order, Mr Latimer?'

Her hands were already sliding upwards, her body swaying forward, closing the gap between them.

The long kiss resolved a great deal, but not everything.

When Dean had put her gently away from him because it was not the time or the place to abandon all restraint, she said, 'One letter in all that time... and not the love letter I was longing for.'

'I was setting up the deal for Manik... giving him a chance. I like Manik—he's a good guy. It seemed right to even the odds.'

'But surely you must have known it was you I loved?' queried Charlotte.

'It seemed to me that you might love us both. I didn't want him to feel that I had an unfair advantage. He's in love with you. If I hadn't happened along you would have been very happy with him.'

'Perhaps... but you did happen along. Surely after that afternoon in my cabin you can't have been in much doubt that it was you I loved more... much, much more.'

'Enough to give up your career?' he asked. 'I've been reading your dossier. You have an excellent record... hard-working, very ambitious. But I want a full-time wife.'

Charlotte smiled. 'Until I met you, I was aiming for a seat on the board, no less. But that was because I had more or less given up hope of falling in love. I've always thought marriage is by far the most demanding career a woman can tackle. But first you have to find the right man. Now that I have, I'll resign my job whenever you say.'

They were married by special licence the following week. It was a small, quiet wedding in the presence of Dean's mother, a few of his closest friends and, on Charlotte's side—so she thought—Sally and Kay and the middle-aged cousin and his wife with whom she had lodged in the school holidays after her grandfather's death.

Out of courtesy she had felt obliged to ask her cousin to give her away. But, when she entered the church on his arm, his wife and Charlotte's two flatmates were not the only people on the bride's side of the aisle.

Beaming at her, as she walked down the aisle in the beautiful dress Maris Richmond Latimer had insisted on buying for her, were the friends she had made on board *Sea Bird*.

Afterwards there was an informal party at Maris's lovely house in Chelsea until, at four o'clock, the bridal couple left in Dean's car for their honeymoon.

Charlotte, who didn't yet know where they were going, thought they might be heading for Heathrow or Gatwick. But although they set out in a direction which might have led to either airport, it was soon clear their destination lay on a route south of Heathrow and west of Gatwick.

'It was fun seeing the others again,' she said, as the luxurious car purred smoothly out of the city. 'It's extraordinary how quickly strangers become friends when they're thrown together on a small boat. Did the Neasdens decline, or didn't you ask them?'

'I didn't think any of us would miss Stanley. Olly looked a knock-out in that pink get-up, didn't she?' said Dean.

'It's her Ascot outfit. Vic took her to Ascot for their twenty-fifth wedding anniversary. Janet's blue hat was bought last week for their middle son's wedding in May. Diane surprised me. I expected something way out, but her dress was almost conservative. Must be the Professor's influence. They've seen each other several times since they got back, she tells me.'

They discussed the wedding and their guests until Charlotte said, 'I think I know where we're going...to your cottage?'

'Disappointed?' he asked.

'Not a bit. I've been longing to see it.'

'As we'll be travelling a lot in the next forty-odd years, it seemed a good idea to start our marriage somewhere quiet, comfortable and not far away. Mrs Dollis, who looks after the place for me, will have lit the fire and stocked the fridge. She won't reappear until Tuesday.' He took one hand off the wheel and laid it lightly on her thigh. 'I shall have you all to myself.'

The following morning Charlotte woke up in a high old-fashioned bed from which she could see as well as hear the river which had once driven the great mill-wheel from which the cottage took its name.

She was alone. The window, open during the night while they slept in each other's arms under a goose-down duvet, had been closed. But the thumb-latched plank door was now ajar. From the kitchen came the sounds of breakfast being prepared and of Dean whistling.

Naked, Charlotte slipped out of bed and padded across one of the Turkish and Persian rugs collected by his grandfather to the adjoining bathroom. She was back

in bed, teeth and hair brushed, when he returned with
a tray.

'Good morning, Mrs Latimer. How did you sleep?'

'Better than I've ever slept before.'

'Me too.'

He put the tray on the chest of drawers next to the
bed and leaned over to kiss her, the front of his white
terry bathrobe loosening to show his hard, still lightly
tanned chest.

Charlotte coiled one arm round his neck and slipped
her other hand inside his robe until it was pressed to the
warm brown skin over his heart.

'I'll remember last night all my life. It was wonderful,' she murmured, lifting her mouth for his kiss.

Dean gathered her into his arms. The breakfast tray
stood forgotten; coffee and toast growing cold as the
sun rose higher and the mist veiling the water-meadows
on the far bank of the river evaporated.

Later, lying with her head on his shoulder, Charlotte
watched the reflections of sunlight on moving water
shimmering on the ceiling. They reminded her of the
sparkling reflections of the sea on *Sea Bird*'s white hull,
and of the man whose dark, aloof face was also im-
printed on her memory. Suddenly her deep contentment
was pierced by a thrust of regret, not because she would
never lie in his arms but because he had yet to find—
might never find—his true love.

Dean said quietly, 'Are you thinking about Manik?'

'Yes...I was. How did you know?' Would the truthful
answer make him angry?

He withdrew his arm from beneath her and, raising
himself on one elbow, looked down into her face.

'The lights on the ceiling were reminding me of the
schooner. It wasn't hard to guess where that track would
lead you. Manik was your first love. He'll always have

a corner of your heart—I understand that. For me, the important thing is to be your last love.'

'You will be,' she told him softly. 'I believe I knew the first time I saw you, at Heathrow, that you were the love of my life. There was something...hard to explain...a kind of recognition. But it obviously wasn't mutual. You didn't even notice me at the airport, and when I spoke to you at Nairobi you were very offhand.'

'For which you'll never quite forgive me,' he said, with a smile.

'Oh, I think I might, given time.' She turned her head towards the window. 'It's going to be a lovely day. Let's get up and have breakfast and then you can show me your village...our village.'

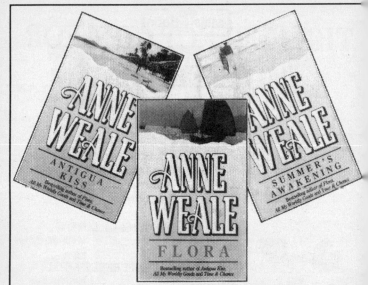

BY THE SAME AUTHOR

ANTIGUA KISS £3.99

Ash Lambard offered Christiana escape with a life in the sun on a lovely Caribbean island. He also offered her marriage. Christiana agreed to become his wife – but on certain conditions. Ash accepted her terms, until their wedding night when she found he'd no intention of keeping his word.

FLORA £3.99

A delicate Eurasian beauty who moved between two worlds, but was shunned by both. An innocent whose awakened fires could be ignited by only one man. This sensuous tale sweeps from remotest China to the decadence of old Shanghai, reaching its heart-stirring conclusion in the opulent Longwarden mansion and lush estates of Edwardian England.

SUMMER'S AWAKENING £3.99

A life-long battle had kept Summer Roberts isolated and insecure. Computer tycoon James Gardiner's entry into her sheltered world was devastating in more ways than one. Through his kindness and unintentional cruelty she emerged a slender, beautiful woman – sure of herself, and sure of her love.

W❂RLDWIDE

4 FREE

Romances
and 2 FREE gifts
just for you!

*You can enjoy all the
heartwarming emotion of true love for FREE!
Discover the heartbreak and the happiness, the emotion and
the tenderness of the modern relationships in
Mills & Boon Romances.*

*We'll send you 4 captivating Romances as a special offer from
Mills & Boon Reader Service, along with the chance to have
6 Romances delivered to your door each month.*

Claim your FREE books and gifts overleaf...

An irresistible offer from Mills & Boon

Here's a personal invitation from Mills & Boon Reader Service, to become a regular reader of Romances. To welcome you, we'd like you to have 4 books, a CUDDLY TEDDY and a special MYSTERY GIFT absolutely FREE.

Then you could look forward each month to receiving 6 brand new Romances, delivered to your door, postage and packing free! Plus our free Newsletter featuring author news, competitions, special offers and much more.

This invitation comes with no strings attached. You may cancel or suspend your subscription at any time, and still keep your free books and gifts.

It's so easy. Send no money now. Simply fill in the coupon below and post it to -
**Reader Service, FREEPOST,
PO Box 236, Croydon, Surrey CR9 9EL.**

NO STAMP REQUIRED

Free Books Coupon

Yes! Please rush me 4 free Romances and 2 free gifts! Please also reserve me a Reader Service subscription. If I decide to subscribe I can look forward to receiving 6 brand new Romances each month for just £10.20, postage and packing free. If I choose not to subscribe I shall write to you within 10 days - I can keep the books and gifts whatever I decide. I may cancel or suspend my subscription at any time. I am over 18 years of age.

Ms/Mrs/Miss/Mr_____ EP31R

Address_____

_____

Postcode_____Signature_____

Mills & Boon

Next Month's Romances

Each month you can choose from a wide variety of romance with Mills & Boon. Below are the new titles to look out for next month, why not ask either Mills & Boon Reader Service or your Newsagent to reserve you a copy of the titles you want to buy — just tick the titles you would like and either post to Reader Service or take it to any Newsagent and ask them to order your books.

Please save me the following titles:	Please tick	√
BREAKING POINT	Emma Darcy	
SUCH DARK MAGIC	Robyn Donald	
AFTER THE BALL	Catherine George	
TWO-TIMING MAN	Roberta Leigh	
HOST OF RICHES	Elizabeth Power	
MASK OF DECEPTION	Sara Wood	
A SOLITARY HEART	Amanda Carpenter	
AFTER THE FIRE	Kay Gregory	
BITTERSWEET YESTERDAYS	Kate Proctor	
YESTERDAY'S PASSION	Catherine O'Connor	
NIGHT OF THE SCORPION	Rosemary Carter	
NO ESCAPING LOVE	Sharon Kendrick	
OUTBACK LEGACY	Elizabeth Duke	
RANSACKED HEART	Jayne Bauling	
STORMY REUNION	Sandra K. Rhoades	
A POINT OF PRIDE	Liz Fielding	

If you would like to order these books in addition to your regular subscription from Mills & Boon Reader Service please send £1.70 per title to: Mills & Boon Reader Service, P.O. Box 236, Croydon, Surrey, CR9 3RU, quote your Subscriber No:............................... (If applicable) and complete the name and address details below. Alternatively, these books are available from many local Newsagents including W.H.Smith, J.Menzies, Martins and other paperback stockists from 12th March 1993.

Name:..

Address:..

....Post Code:..........................

To Retailer: If you would like to stock M&B books please contact your regular book/magazine wholesaler for details.